Igor Sakhnovsky

THE VITAL NEEDS OF THE DEAD

Glagoslav Publications

The Vital Needs Of The Dead
By Igor Sakhnovsky

First published in Russian as
"Насущные нужды умерших. Хроника"

Translated by Julia Kent
Edited by Nina Chordas

© 2012, Glagoslav Publications, United Kingdom

Glagoslav Publications Ltd
88-90 Hatton Garden
EC1N 8PN London
United Kingdom

www.glagoslav.com

ISBN: 978-1-909156-17-3

Contents

A Chronicle

My relationship with this woman resembles the parched proverbial link between a slave oarsman and the galley that is chained to him. However, in our case one could argue about who is chained to whom, the more so because even when she was alive – and also afterwards – we had to take each other's place more than once. Particularly afterwards.

I am not used to saying out loud her name which is florid and slightly embarrassing, for I never, not once, addressed her by her name.

She had the same surname as me, which is Sidelnikov. She was Rosa Sidelnikov. For a long time this quite mundane fact seemed to me an inexplicable coincidence.

What is hardest for me now is to speak about her in the third person. A doctor who comes to visit a terminally ill or mentally unstable patient, asks the confused relatives in a business-like manner, 'Has he been sweating like this all the time? What has his stool been like?' Or he enquires with lazy furtiveness but audibly enough, 'Has he stopped screaming about the attempts on his life? Well, you'd better not remind him.' The family stunned by hopelessness and fear naturally reply in the desired key. And then the fleeting reek of betrayal permeates the medicinal stuffiness of the room. Henceforth, the human being in question is defeated in his last remaining rights. The loved and cherished "you" disappears forever from that clammy hateful bed and only "he" remains, abandoned to its own devices.

Calling Rosa "she" now, I can hear the condescending silence of a person present but detached from us all by the same status of complete incurability – or "insanity". Except that her illness is simply called death.

CHAPTER ONE

After so many other Augusts that have rolled away yonder like overripe apples, those particular August nights and days continue to glow and their radiance hurts my eyes. Here is my first memory of Rosa, my earliest naked and nocturnal recollection of her.

The day was ending, inopportunely as usual. I never felt sleepy and perceived the night as a forced interruption of the breathtaking life of the day.

Rosa made her bed on a narrow couch, covered with black leatherette, and then made my bed on an iron bedstead by the opposite wall. Whilst undressing, I was absentmindedly listening to the garrulous life of our neighbours. Beyond the thin partition of the shared flat, the large Baronkin family was getting ready for bed.

Their settling for the night was as long and thorough as if they were seeing themselves off on a long journey. The head of the family, Vassily, was giving the final evening instructions to his wife Tatyana. Every now and then, their children, with their bare heels pounding on the floor, would run to them with detailed reports and complaints about each other. Every other minute, Vassily would put in the short, only four letters long, yet pithy expletive denoting the utter hopelessness of everything. Incidentally, it was the same word which, since the end of last summer, anybody wishing to do so could see written in enormous letters inscribed in tar on the yellow stucco facade of their two-storey block of flats in Shkiryatov street.

Flushed after washing her face, Rosa was brushing her hair in front of the mirror with the moulded institutional frame. That rectangular mirror, on the wall next to the window, seemed to me a second window that was also open, although not out into the yard but inside, from out of the yard full of darkness into Rosa's half-empty and brightly lit room.

I had already got under the woollen blanket and was listening to the neighbours' radio, big-heartedly blaring out the Saturday request concert. "This song is to honour a beloved weaver, decorated with an Order, a mother and a grandmother who unselfishly gave up many years of her life." The singer had the voice of crazy red-haired Lydia who lived on the ground floor:

> *Oh Samara, little town,*
> *I am restless, oh so restless!*
> *Would you calm me down!*

Without turning, Rosa suddenly enquired whether I was hungry. I was imagining how the little town of Samara would rush as fast as its legs would carry it to calm down the unsettled imbecile. No, I wasn't hungry. By the way, Lydia from the ground floor was quite placid and did not require any calming down. For days on end, she strolled to and fro in the yard in a faded loose-fitting sundress that was very cute, but for some reason always had a hideous greasy stain underneath her belly.

Then it was some sullen robust fellow's turn to sing:

> *There were only three of us*
> *Left out of eighteen lads.*
> *How many of them fell...*

After Tatyana's heavyish steps, the radio shut up abruptly and Vassily pronounced his farewell "a-ha, he, he-he he-he!" and then all the Baronkins, as it were, instantly departed.

In this brand-new space of stillness, Rosa's and my silence at once became clearly discernible, our usual and not at all burdensome solitude of the two of us together. One could say that we almost did not take notice of each other - which is the everyday lot of the most needed people and things when they are constantly next to you.

Rosa always slept naked and she made me used to doing the same. I liked her habits. I knew that in the next moment after the dry rustle of her palms rubbing in the cream from the bottle with the inscription "Velvety" and after the click of the switch, I would hear, 'Go to sleep, dear,' uttered with her inimitable cool and crisp intonation, and even before my eyes became used to darkness, she would pull the house-dress over her head and quietly lie down on the narrow sloping couch.

'Go to sleep, dear.'

Igor Sakhnovsky

But the darkness and silence would not come. My reluctance to sleep was encouraged by the cicadas trilling with such demented intensity that their shrill chorus came literally crashing through the narrow opening of the window. The whole room was flooded with luminous lunar juice. In the middle, the oilcloth on the dining table shone like a little round pond. The walls turned into screens for a night film-show starring the yard's two largest hackberry trees. A bulky shadow was snuggling in the corner by the wardrobe; his back split by the border between the wall and the ceiling, his head hanging dejectedly on a thin neck. Opposite him, almost on the floor, another shadow sat heavily, stocky and immersed in himself. From time to time, there was the sound of a gusty, leafy inhalation and at that instant, the stooping one would fly out of his corner with clumsy determination in order to fall down on his knees before the seated one. But each time the latter would move away imperviously and it was only during the exhalation that both returned to their original positions. This desperate scene would repeat itself over and over again and no-one could foresee how it might end. The tall shadow was still hoping to obtain pardon by his pleading and continued to prostrate himself at the other's feet. I was waiting in hope that the short one would at last relent or at least would not be able to move away quickly enough, but he was always on the alert...

There were two questions I had to mull over which were almost a secret. In any case, there was nobody I could turn to in order to discuss them.

First, I noticed that if I screwed up my eyes a little, either in the light or in the darkness, my eyes would turn into something like a microscope and I could immediately see an innumerable multitude of tiny round creatures in transparent shells, with minuscule nuclei inside. They were always on the move, sometimes as if reluctant and sometimes fast, closely surrounded by even tinier creatures, also diaphanous and shimmering. All in all, the whole air (if I could believe my screwed up eyes) was replete with these small fry who lived their own, mysterious lives. But discerning any details of that life was beyond my powers. I decided to entrust this task to scientists, should they ever become interested in the peculiarity of my vision. A special device must be invented to enable the scientists to observe with my eyes from inside of me the creatures that I had discovered. Anyhow, thinking about the scientists was boring and I turned to the other conundrum.

Actually, this other question was puzzling me much more. I needed to understand – who on earth was Rosa? I just realised that I knew almost nothing about this woman. She doesn't seem to have any friends. She doesn't go to work. She lives alone in this square room with bare walls. In her plywood wardrobe painted with floor paint, there are hangers with two or three dresses and a coat. On the whatnot in the same colour as the wardrobe, there is a radio that looks like a military transmitter and a pile of literary monthlies from the town library. She has neither a fridge nor a television, nor a little rug depicting a seated beauty, nor portraits on the walls like those that the Baronkins could boast of (yet they always complain to each other about lack of money). Compared with them, Rosa in my opinion is very poor, almost destitute.

But she never complains about anything and, on the whole, talks very little.

The most perplexing part is her attitude towards me, her silent, constant and dogged care that is simply inexplicable. Calmly and diligently, she watches over my wellbeing and the correctness of my every move, and it seems that there was or is no other purpose in her life.

I suddenly felt hot. The scratchy blanket was burning my skin. The odd expression "watches over" got stuck in my head and grew a sinister sprout: "watches over – by order". So, does it mean that… somebody must have secretly chosen me to be their tool… and Rosa is entrusted with leading and directing me towards the required purpose? What would she do if I spoke my thoughts aloud? Most likely she would…

At that moment, I was so startled that I bit my lip. Something white flickered in the dark abyss of the mirror aslant from me, and another shadow rose between the two which kept scurrying over the wall.

But in an instant, it became clear to me that Rosa had risen from her bed and was moving towards me. Her face was shaded by thick darkness, yet her body, smooth and thin, was almost translucent in the night's silvery glow. Barely having time to shut my eyes, I felt the wave of air, warmed by her body and, through my lowered eyelashes, saw a small sinuous belly right in front of me. It was shaded by her breasts, which looked like two tall pitchers.

Why does this long gone uneventful night continue to beam so powerfully the radioactive rays of terror and rapture that reach and affect my present self? Indeed, can one seriously, without a smile, elevate to the rank of an event a thing like that: one person's getting up in the middle of the night and coming up to the bed of another person, lifting the blanket that dropped on the floor and covering the one lying in bed telling him with a gentle chuckle, 'C'mon, stop fretting, sleep well...'

However, everything that happened then and afterwards has turned into a chain of irrefutable proofs making me admit that there is nothing more frightening, beautiful and fantastical than so-called *real* life. This very life, banal yet particular, essentially languishing in numbness and obscurity, desires to entrust itself to words, whereas words are mostly concerned with their appearance and are always preening.

When I started telling this story, I made a promise to myself not to give in to the temptation to invent things and at the very least not to make up any circumstances, as long as those still alive and uninvented, and virtually impossible to invent, are waiting to be noticed, like poor relations pining by the door all this time.

I turned over to the other side, face to the wall, listening to her barefoot steps and realising that, during all the time of my vigil, Rosa was not asleep either. It was as if she had listened to me and then given a cautious and accurate reply to my loud delirious thoughts, which very soon, in just fifteen years or even less, would turn out not so delirious at all.

CHAPTER TWO

At the Baronkins, Sunday morning started in the tempo of a vigorous squabble that came to the boil in sync with Tatyana's pea soup.

Trousered but bare-chested, Vassily was fretfully pacing the shared flat's corridor now and again filling the cramped communal space with clamour on the sore subject:

'Who da fuck is da boss in 'ere?'

Tatyana kept silent and did not take her eyes off the stove.

At that same time, sprawling on the unmade bed of her parents, Lisa, one of the Baronkin twins, was interrogating the other twin sitting by her side:

'Olga, you are a mongol, aren't you? Tell me honestly!'

And without waiting for an answer, she announced:

'I know, you're a mongol. Mum told me. I am going to tell everybody that you're a mongol.'

Olga suddenly broke into a howl, covering her face with her fists, whereupon Lisa decided to temper justice with mercy:

'Hey, don't shit your pants! Okay, I won't tell then!'

Olga the mongol would not stop. Her howling woke up and frightened her younger brothers.

Tatyana cocked an ear to the discordant wailing of her children and replied sullenly to her husband's next query as to who da fuck was da boss in 'ere:

'The cockroaches.'

Rosa had put on an old-fashioned bathing suit under her frock. It meant that on this day she and Sidelnikov might visit the beach, unless the weather turned foul.

But the weather seemed to have forgotten its own existence. The town looked southern and indolent like some resort, although in actual fact it was an industrial town in the mid-Urals.

Sidelnikov and Rosa were going down the deserted street formerly known as Shkiryatov. It had recently been renamed Oil Workers' Street but the new name had not yet managed to take root.

Sidelnikov interrupted their habitual silence by asking Rosa why the street was renamed. It cannot be stated for certain that he was very interested in the question, but still... Rosa slightly winced, letting him see that it was of even less interest to her but, after some hesitation, said something along the lines of, well, you see, this Shkiryatov fellow turned out to be a bad man all of a sudden.

Sidelnikov made an attempt at a witty remark:

'What if afterwards it turns out that the oil workers are baddies, too?'

Rosa did not appreciate the joke and gave him an unexpectedly serious reply:

'They ought to be spared: they've already had their share of being called bad.'

With that, the conversation fizzled out. However, Sidelnikov was still a bit sorry for the old name because he fancied that it had some awe-inspiring gangster charm. One day, donkey's years later, the abolished name would surface and merge on paper with an indescribably ugly mug, of the kind one would only expect in a nightmare. Sidelnikov, rummaging in a second-hand book shop, would find and take into his hands a shiny book with biographies of those honoured enough to be buried near the Kremlin Wall, or in the Wall itself. From a page opened by providence, an affectionate cannibal smile would be bestowed upon him by a functionary with bovine eyes set at the width of his iron-cast cheekbones: the unforgettable Matvey Shkiryatov.

But right at this moment, it was just a street where Rosa lived, where the inevitable imminent joy was trying – and failing – to hide behind the provinciality of the place and motionlessness of the time, and the shabby luxury of the pending Sunday walk. It was for this joy and to serve this joy that everything they encountered on their way was created.

Well, first of all, they would come across the Haberdashery Store. It was impossible not to nip in there. It was called "to go have a glance at the diamonds". It is true that Rosa preferred the counter with cottons and buttons (where hardly anything caught the eye), but Sidelnikov straightaway glued himself to the counters where the "jewels" were displayed. The sun just about managed to squeeze itself through the grimy shop window and regained its strength on the display, thanks to the magnificent, like oil on water, iridescent splash fragmented into large faceted shards, priced about two roubles apiece. There also were swimming and shimmering bottle green and wine-red glassy treasures of such depth and clarity that they surely could be nothing but emeralds and rubies. These beauties never diminished since nobody ever bought them. Anyway, the idea that the treasure could be bought by anyone, taken in hand and put into a pocket never crossed Sidelnikov's mind. The impression was enhanced by the divine redolence of "Carmen" face powder and "Chypre" eau-de-cologne.

After these haberdashery refinements, the air and the light in the street appeared bland and faded. But this did not mean to cause disappointment. The day was still there – with an open face whose every feature was a firm promise of a fabulous future that could not be cancelled.

The evidence was manifesting itself: the yell of a woman who had wandered from the suburbs with heavy milk cans ('Milk, any-o-o-one?'); the cheerfulness of a short-legged stray dog met on the way; Rosa's nimble step; and finally at the turning into Lenin Avenue, the billboards advertising "The Queen of the Filling Station" and "The Return of Veronica" at the "Mir" cinema. From those obscure names Sidelnikov contrived to glean a lot more than could possibly be crammed into any, even the most mind-blowing, film.

Everything he saw provoked his hunger and thirst - the dogberry bushes in the middle of the lawn, the rainbow running obediently in the spray of the street cleaning machine or the insistent inscription on a shop window: "If you want to be beautiful, be it!" If at that moment somebody were to ask Sidelnikov whether there was anything he did not want he would not have been able to give an answer. Because he wanted *everything*. The more pleasurable was the torment of his silent reserve, encouraged by the secret pact with Rosa.

Indeed, there was nothing strange in the fact that, upon entering the nearest grocery store, Rosa would immediately buy Sidelnikov a glass of tomato juice that cost 10 kopecks, without even asking whether he felt like it or not. While the shop assistant, having turned the minuscule faucet, was slowly dispensing the trickling juice out of a tall conical glass container, Sidelnikov fished an aluminium teaspoon out of a jar filled with water in order to scratch for and obtain some petrified salt out of another jar. He clinked for a long time stirring the salt in his glass and then sank the spoon in the jar where the water was turning pink, and then, at last, got a mouthful of the fresh grassy coolness. It was the tiny crystals of the undissolved salt on the bottom of the glass that always turned out the most delicious of all.

Still with his moustache of red juice, Sidelnikov grabbed hold of the tiny parcel of low fat "doctor's" sausage that was bought for him just then and would be devoured by him in an instant.

Well, the sausage was gone – and why dwell on it? Yet one ought to mention the fabled age when boiled sausage priced two roubles twenty kopecks per kilo would become an object of deep preoccupation for the population of this huge country. And Sidelnikov, who by that time would have moved to another, larger city, would learn to woo the arrogant salesgirls. Suppressing the spasms of gentility-born queasiness, he would wheedle one or two extra sausage batons (over and above the allowed ration), in order to be able afterwards to transport victoriously those congealed treasures in a second-class carriage to his home town in the Southern Urals. The people there had almost forgotten the taste of the said victual, despite the concerted working efforts of the local meat processing factory. Rosa would not live to see those cruel times.

...

The central square was as quiet and forlorn as any other part of the town. By the newsstand, a fat woman in an apron was melting, glued to her candyfloss stall. For a three-kopeck bribe, several vending machines the colour of fire engines were ready for anything: to spray up to the ears whoever would dare plunge his hand into their white innards; or to spurt up a faceted glass full of prickly water with syrup; or yet to retain proud silence - surely, one could not possibly spurt every single time!

The main adornment of the square was provided by the ruins of the prospective drama theatre, a lethargic construction site thanks to which a whole generation of citizens was able to answer calls of their modest nature not just anywhere in the bushes, but behind reliable red brick walls. A few years later, this square would be renamed Komsomol Square, and into a low cement barrier by the ruins there would be immured, in the presence of an enormous congregation of gloomy schoolchildren, a Message To Progeny with an oath of loyalty to Lenin's Party alongside other urgent communications.

Number Four tram came rolling to the stop, tinkling every now and again.

'Is this ours?' Sidelnikov asked anxiously, thus starting the game of pretending to be newly arrived in town, and maybe even a foreigner.

'This is our tram', Rosa, the local resident, assured him.

Sidelnikov, as a guest, sat by the window and Rosa rode standing, as if ignoring the vacant seats. The lady tram driver announced the stops regularly, like news headlines: "Vanguard stadium", "Machinery Plant"...

'Is this a machinery plant?' the "foreigner", clearly a little bit dense, liked to make certain.

'Yes it is', Rosa replied, looking down at him, for some reason with fondness.

The crude plaster figures of the man and woman toilers near the "Hammer and Sickle" Palace of Culture were shining as if made from pure silver. They too received their portion of attention paid as intently as if they were seen for the first time.

It must be mentioned that all tram routes in the town terminated at railway stations (of which there were two). And it stood to reason that all other stops, such as, for instance, "Collective Farm Market" or "River Ural" appeared something auxiliary and intermediary on the approach to the ideal final goal embodied in the railway stations. It was the stations, reeking of soot and toilet bleach that played the role of some magic lens beaming out rays of unpredictable paths and opportunities.

The river divided the town in two: the new part, as yet unfinished but already priming itself to become the main part, thanks to the precocious five-storied blocks of flats, and the so-called Old Town that became undisputedly famous for two reasons. First, it was here that the Ukrainian national (and obviously for that reason punished by the czarist system) poet Tarass Shevchenko was exiled, or, simply speaking, where he served in the army. Evidence survived as to how badly he was suffering here. He was forever pulling at his fashionable moustache and was sighing in his native Ukrainian tongue, 'No-h-one would weeep... No-h-one would weeep!' The second, if not the main, reason for the well-deserved fame of the Old Town, was the Old Town fried offal pasties. They were unique, that is, incomparable to anything at all in terms of taste and aroma. The pasties were so well-loved by the locals that at weekends they would not consider it beneath themselves to form a mile-long queue; while during the working week they would send an emissary representing a whole team or a workshop to the coveted steaming stall by the bridge. And the aroma from the left bank was so far-reaching that it made those living on the right bank either sit salivating, or promptly cross the river by the tram over the bridge and join the tail of the endless queue.

Sidelnikov was especially impressed by the fact that the river was once and for all declared The Official Border between Europe and Asia by someone from above. Therefore, before taking off his shoes on the hot wet sand, Sidelnikov would first peruse the opposite bank with curiosity and even certain angst, striving to spot the natives: 'How are they doing over there? They are in Asia, after all!'

Meanwhile, the river was rivalling the sky in its blinding shine and speed. It was streaming past the heat-worn beach, needing nobody and nothing.

Rosa touched the water with a wary bronzed foot and then strolled for some time along the wet strip of the beach. Walking, she was unhurriedly tidying her hair away under a light-coloured, sun-bleached bandanna.

Igor Sakhnovsky

It was the season of tiny bluish-black dragonflies that appeared out of nowhere, in order to gaze at people in silence and hang above the water. They suddenly flew all together to Rosa, the whole mica-sparkling gaggle of them, as cordially as if they recognised her to be a relative. For some reason, Rosa accepted it for granted and did not even brush away the most passionate ones when they landed on her breast, which made her tan seem paler and her skin vulnerably white.

Unable to match her pace Sidelnikov was feeling self-conscious and scurried around, intercepting the sunbathers' stares at Rosa and vexed by the dragonflies' circus, which clearly was what attracted the attention of the bored men.

Then, into the bargain, Innokenty materialised in the flesh, as if he had been deliberately lying in wait for Rosa in order to, as usual, strike up a conversation with her in his at once wounded and adoring voice. And he always just failed to notice Sidelnikov, or looked through him.

Swimming did not appeal. The only thing left to Sidelnikov was to walk back by himself to the blue counterpane which had been spread on the sand by Rosa and to lie down to sunbathe. While scanning the feathery heavens for a short time, deliberately trying to imagine that it was not the heavens, but, on the contrary, a vertiginous bottomless pit, Sidelnikov noticed, by lateral vision, two pairs of wet legs: a hirsute one with sand stuck up to the ankles, as if covered in mustard plaster, and an immaculately clean one shimmering with tiny silvery sparkles.

'It's a shame that you can't see yourself from the outside,' Rosa's cool voice was sympathising.

'Well, I've quite forgotten what I look like. Before you know it, I'll forget what my name is,' Innokenty was replying quite seriously. 'It's been four months now that I can't sleep at night, and during the day I feel happy and silly as a boy.'

'Well, you are a boy.'

'Rosa, I am nearly forty,' confessed Innokenty, exercising a complicated manoeuvre with his right foot in order to get the sand off his left. It seemed that he was priming himself for a daring move, and then at last he ventured:

'May I come and visit you sometime?'

Sidelnikov was sure that Rosa would reply, 'Get away!' to him and even felt sorry for Innokenty, who froze on one leg in apprehension.

But unexpectedly, she said:

'It's my birthday on Wednesday. Would you come by around six? The only thing is, I'm not going to celebrate and I do not want any presents. And you'll need my address...'

'I know the address!' Innokenty cried hoarsely and broke into a cough. Then he took an awkward pause during which the situation on the cloud front changed completely and then, obviously at a loss for words, he offered solicitously:

'Shall I remove this dragonfly off you?'

'Get away!' said Rosa.

In the evening of the same day, taking advantage of Rosa's absence, Sidelnikov got out of the whatnot's drawer an ink pot, a school nib attached to a wooden handle, and a pack of greeting cards in which he found one that was clean and uninscribed. On the front, a powerful fist was depicted, clutching a bunch of flowers with a vague interpretation offered underneath: "Peace. Labour. Month of May".

He perched on the edge of the table, poked the ink pot with the nib and on the reverse of the card, scribbled painstakingly the first word:

Nana!

He thought a little, and then just as painstakingly crossed out the word and wrote above it on the left:

Dearest!

The word "Dearest" came out a bit askew but the lines that followed were appearing better aligned:

Happy birthday to you.
I wish for you to be free of any illness,
to be merry and to live until ...

Here Sidelnikov fell into a reverie. He was not happy about what he had written so far yet he did not feel like crossing out anything anymore. The nib dried up and started to resemble the back of a golden beetle.

All right. 'To live until ...' Suddenly, he felt as if he were a bestower of infinite beneficence and, upon a momentary musing, inserted an almost fantastical date into the greetings:

... until 1975!

Overwhelmed by good feelings, Sidelnikov bolstered the concluding exclamation mark with more ink, waved the card dry and took it along the corridor to the mailbox attached to the inside of the front door.

He had done his part. On returning to the room, he headed straight to the window: Rosa, alive and merry and free from any illness, was standing in the middle of the yard talking with the crazy redhead Lydia. He could not make out any words. At that moment Lydia might have appeared a lady of consequence – if only she were not scratching her greasy underbelly, now with the right hand, now with the left.

The August of the unforgettable year nineteen sixty-four was running out. In the previous month, Sidelnikov entered the seventh year of his life. In two days time, Rosa would turn fifty. She would have exactly eleven years more to live

CHAPTER THREE

The enemy was attacking continuously, now in infantry, now in cavalry formations, and it was only owing to his colossal courage that Sidelnikov was managing to fight off one attack after another. He had already been lying prone in the trench for half an hour. His shoulders and legs got numb but he continued to return fire.

A new detachment was approaching. Of course, it was the Tartars again. In order to terrify Sidelnikov they shaved their heads clean, they were brandishing their colourful lashes and shouting 'Hurrah!' in Tartar. Their only aim was to capture

Maria, to put her forcibly on a horse and take her to Khan Girei's harem. There, in his harem, Khan Girei would be able to ogle in any way and even touch her beauty – again, by force. That is how it would have happened – were it not for Sidelnikov.

Maria was lying next to him, aswoon from fright. She was completely helpless and so puny that she easily fitted on the edge of the couch, alias the trench, between the leatherette bolster and the elbow of her saviour. At the height of battle, hoarse from the loud machine-gun rounds, he would sometimes have a moment to fondle Maria, looming with his huge torso over her defenceless little body. Doing this, Sidelnikov would suddenly catch himself turning a little bit into Khan Girei, who resembled a black eagle. And although Maria was lying there wholly unconscious and actually was completely invisible, Sidelnikov himself was very visible during those moments and was slightly apprehensive that the maiden might notice this strange split in his personality and the totally out-of-place, shameful tension in his mended tight shorts.

A few days previously, Sidelnikov's parents, who were forever either busy at work or engaged in sorting out their uneasy relationship, owing to the difference in their temperaments, all of a sudden made a short truce and remembered their half-wit son Gosha. They even got round to bringing him home for an evening from Granny Rosa (likewise half-witted, as a matter of fact), in order to take him with them to the Machine Builders' Palace of Culture to see "The Fountain of Bakhchisarai", performed by a touring ballet troupe. Such outings happened only once in several years, but for Sidelnikov it was the first time ever. So he had his reasons to worry and tread on the grown-ups' shoes and ask them silly questions. They would cut him short angrily but he sensed in any case that all this festivity and his mother's black and white polka dot dress, her smiling nervousness, the sharp sickly waves of her "Red Moscow" scent, his father's starched cuffs and unusual good humour were presents, splendid but in no way deserved and surely not his to keep.

It turned out that an orchestra could play other than at a funeral, and much better and more frightening at that, even though at the time Sidelnikov could not imagine anything more frightening than a funeral band. However, on this occasion he found out that music was not responsible for death alone. It participated in everything, rather like the weather. The same music made Sidelnikov feel agonising envy and literally fall in love with all and sundry: Maria's fiancé, hacked to death by a sword, and Khan Girei and even the homeliest of the slave girls attired in transparent nylon trousers. Not to mention that maiden, Maria...

The impact was so powerful that Sidelnikov had difficulty surviving till the following morning when he, numb, was taken in silence to the kindergarten where he at last fell greedily upon his audience – the always drowsy Vladik Baranov who had not yet known anything, not anything at all! The account was started at the clothes lockers, was continued during breakfast with the pearl barley gruel in his mouth, and was interrupted by the appearance of Galia Sharipovna, the pretty cleaner who started taking away the dishes and wiping the tables clean. Her arrival was always preceded by the suffocating reek of bleach from the rag she never let out of her hand.

During the walk around the playground shelter with the peeling paint, the eyewitness and well-nigh participant of the Bakhchisarai's events proceeded to describe them anew. He could not afford to miss a single detail. He was narrating the music, emitting inhumanly complicated sounds with hasty side remarks: 'Then they started dancing... Here's dancing... Dancing again...' Vladik Baranov was opening his eyes wider than usual and blinking fast.

All of the most interesting stuff was still untold, but after lunch the boys were parted by the "quiet hour", the daily torture whereby one had to languish under sheets wasting one's time for nothing and envying even the flies that could freely go wherever they wished anytime without having to ask permission.

But after tea, they congregated again, behind the lockers. Children were being picked up to go home and nobody was disturbing the boys. The crucial battle was approaching. And the Tartars flew at full tilt straight into the dancing room! The din of the skirmish and the sound of his own voice rendered Sidelnikov almost deaf. He was not scared, he just closed his eyes for one second – and when he opened his eyes, he saw the face of Galia Sharipovna disfigured by rage. Overpowering the orchestra, she screamed, 'I'll show you the "Tartars"! You little shit!' After the wet rag slapped his face, he could no longer see anything and was not fighting anyone. He was standing, hunched, pressing his head into his shoulders and hiding his face that stunk of bleach in his palms.

There was a desert around him. Beyond it, people could still walk and talk and answer questions of the arriving parents. But that mash of sounds suddenly froze pierced by a voice that was colder than usual, almost icy, and could belong only to Rosa: 'If you... scum... dare to touch him... ever again... I'll have you ... put away.'

Rosa was dragging him by the hand across the yard of the kindergarten but at the gate, he abruptly stopped and tried to wrench his hand out and run back. He suddenly understood everything. The cleaning girl had not seen the show; she did not know what it was about. He should tell her everything! She assumed that he was saying bad things about those who were not Russian. She was hurt! And the wicked Rosa called her "scum"! And the girl was hurt and didn't know... And he...

At this moment he vomited his tea straight down onto his feet and sandals. And his shorts got soiled as well. Rosa started wiping his face but he was fighting back, coughing, and finally started crying. Because nothing, but nothing, could be explained to anybody.

CHAPTER FOUR

Of the time that he lived at Rosa's, Sidelnikov remembered remarkably few days in the same detail as this one, during which the intimate subcurrent of life showed itself with uninvited bluntness.

Igor Sakhnovsky

He learnt to distinguish the private from the formal quite early, before he even knew those words. The world was distinctly divided into two parts, the permitted and the concealed, outlawed, of which one could tell no one. Sometimes, both realms began to converge alarmingly and would even touch each other, and that caused him either dismay or strange rapture. He also happened to make mistakes that completely muddled his already overworked head, closely shorn apart from a short fringe.

For example, he knew exactly that the private word "bogeys" meant snot in the nose, and did not mean anything else. Therefore, if Rosa quietly suggested to him to go get the bogeys out, that meant that it was time to blow his nose properly because his stuffed nostrils would not let him breathe and his handkerchief had disappeared somewhere yet again.

Whereas the ABC that Rosa brought him in order to teach him to read was obviously of official provenance, judging by the soporific pictures which showed a banal mama, washing a window frame, and the inevitable Kremlin towers. That was why Sidelnikov's astonishment caused by the first word he had ever read defied description. It was the word "bogeys". He read it twice syllable by syllable and then raised his eyes to Rosa who was sitting next to him, and asked in embarrassment, 'How come *they* know?'

But that was long ago, long before Sidelnikov became an avid reader of everything he happened to come across. He and Rosa even established a new game whereby, come evening, Rosa would say, as if by the way, 'Looks like Nikita Sergeyevich hasn't spoken to us for some while...' At once, Sidelnikov would spring to his feet, drag a chair into a free space and set it with its back to the audience. He put on the seat a newspaper taken from the window-sill and placed a glass of water nearby, and then in a heavy slow voice borrowed from radio newsreaders announced the heading of the editorial: 'The Speech of Comrade N. S. Khrushchev!' Nearly knocking the glass down onto the floor, he darted off again in order to unearth, in the whatnot drawer, somebody's ancient glasses without lenses and without any sidepieces but with an elastic that really made one's ears stick out. Thus equipped, in the round spectacles and lop-eared, he could now walk to the rostrum slowly, taking his time, and start the delivery of his address.

'Dear comrades!'

From the front row, Rosa was looking at him with solemnity and respect.

'At the present time, our Party is carrying out an extensive programme for the production of fertilisers, development of irrigation is under way, and the level of mechanisation is rising.'

'Is that right? Imagine that!' Rosa did not hide her enthusiasm. It is true, however, that from time to time her face looked aloof and a little embarrassed.

'...It can be said with certainty that agricultural workers will guarantee the level...' Sometimes the speaker stumbled and lost the line he was reading. 'The level... Yes, the level of production that has been set out by the Programme of the Communist Party of the Soviet Union.'

At this moment, one had to sip decorously some water from the glass, the way it was done by all the lecturers who used to speak in the yard agitprop centre before free film shows.

'Would you like some tea?'

'Don't interfere! Engaged in the great creative labour for the construction of the communist society, at the same time we shall not forget for one moment the necessity to fight in order to (there was a pause for the brief picking of the nose) prevent the global nuclear war. And in this, our Party follows the path indicated by V. I. Lenin.'

'Oh my, that's spiffing. Maybe you'd like a pancake?'

The speech lasted very long, for about ten minutes. Whereupon Sidelnikov, somewhat weary, would grow cold towards his undertaking, content with the effect produced. The effect consisted, first of all, in his obtaining a golden foolproof master key that fitted anything at all, as much the intimate primeval bogeys, as the global nuclear war.

This pervasive ability was appreciated for what it was worth even by such an authority as Lisa Baronkin who once convened about six local hoods by the storage sheds and brought Sidelnikov there in order to ask him to read the four-letter word that was inscribed in chalk on the boards. He did what was asked of him with unfeigned modesty but irked by the meagreness of the task and incomprehensibility of the inscription. He waited a little in case there would be any further requests, then departed with dignity and not in the least flattered by the mirth of the congregation. On his way back, the unsatisfied reader's hunger made him for the umpteenth time automatically read the word, which denoted the utter hopelessness of things, on the yellow stucco of their block of flats.

And on the day in question, the same Lisa, taking out of her mouth her forefinger, whose nail had not yet been completely chewed off, offered Sidelnikov prospects of revealing a terrible secret on condition that he would not tell anyone, or else he'd be scum. He swore twice, but she was still dragging him in tow from the corridor and into the kitchen, then to the yard and the back of the storage shed darkly reminding, 'Mind, you'll be scum!' He hesitated, but then had to admit reluctantly that okay, he'd be scum. And then she imparted to him uttering every word with gleeful gusto that *some people! Men and women! Go to bed! Naked!*

'So what?' asked Sidelnikov. 'I…know it too. What, do you sleep in your dress?'

Almost insulted, Lisa inquired whether he were an idiot. Sidelnikov more and more reminded her of her own twin sister Olga, who was just as stupid and a thorough mongol into the bargain.

'Are you an idiot? They sleep with each other!'

'A-ha!' Sidelnikov conceded politely. In actual fact, he remained just as much disappointed and was itching to go back to Rosa's room to the unfinished Thomas Mayne Reid novel.

Now Lisa was trying to catch up with him in order to ascertain her dubious triumph. She was jabbering something about bras but he was not listening, and besides it started to rain. But all of a sudden, one phrase caught him like a poisoned arrow. He even stumbled on the porch and badly knocked his knee. 'You don't know how ashamed they feel!' said Lisa Baronkin, and the words hit him with the cold breeze of true-life mystery. The commonplace necessity of sleeping at night became overshadowed by some particular vague procedure, in which certain people, women and men, had to participate by overcoming their shame.

It was quiet and somehow sad in the room. Rosa made tea for Innokenty. He had of late become a fairly frequent visitor but would still get wildly embarrassed every time when he took out of his briefcase edible offerings in the form of sweetened cakes of cottage cheese or when he was hiding from view his feet in hideous socks under the chair. Rosa and Innokenty were talking in a low voice about someone by the name of Nadezhda Konstantinovna.

Sidelnikov perched on the windowsill with his back to them and opened the thick orange volume on a bookmarked page.

"Roblado gave preferment to the belles of Havannah, and descanted upon the plump, material beauty which is characteristic of the Quadroons."

'Did you really know her?' Innokenty was curious.

'What if I did,' Rosa consented coldly.

"...while the lieutenant expressed his penchant for the small-footed Guadalajxareñas..."

'How come you never told me about it? Do you remember anything special? What was she like?'

Sidelnikov immediately imagined the unknown Nadezhda Konstantinovna as a plump, material beauty, but with small feet.

'She was ill and old and could barely walk.'

'And what was she like as a human being, as a person?'

'Do you really want to know what I think? She was a rare idiot, that's what she was.'

The rain was now lashing the windowpane. Innokenty fell silent, obviously shocked by Rosa's words.

Sidelnikov imagined how Lisa Baronkin as a middle-aged sophisticated lady immersed in memories and queried by her slightly bald admirer, 'Did you know Sidelnikov? What was he like?' would answer with confidence, 'He was a rare idiot, that's what he was.'

'We were allowed to look after her.' It sounded as if Rosa was trying to justify herself. 'I was twenty-something, a student at the Bauman University. In those days, I understood nothing at all. But very soon afterwards, I started to. One should avoid such people like the plague.'

'But she was the wife of...'

'The widow. So much the worse for her.'

'I don't mean that,' Innokenty said heatedly but in lowered voice nonetheless. 'I'll never believe that Vladimir Ilyich could be with such, eh, what you called her.'

Sidelnikov froze because it dawned on him who they were talking about.

'Listen,' Rosa said, very sternly. 'Go talk about your Vladimir Ilyich to somebody else. Do you understand?'

The silence that ensued after these words lasted so long that Sidelnikov wanted to turn his head but restrained himself.

'Half my life, I've been not living but hiding in my own country. When before the war they took

Mikhail away, I was chasing all those officials and writing letters. And then one day a friend of mine, who was married to a security officer, dragged me into the loo. She locked the door and whispered to me, so quietly I could hardly hear her, that they were going to take me away any day now and that I was on their list and must flee at once, anywhere as far as possible from Moscow. I still had a chance to look her husband in the eye though he wouldn't look straight in mine. On the next day, I told my neighbours some tall story, rushed to the station with Fedya in my arms and got into a second-class carriage. The rest isn't interesting at all. And I don't feel like recalling it.'

'Anything that concerns you is of interest to me.'

'...When they took Mikhail away, he said goodbye to me as if he were going away on business for a week. We had already been separated at the time, you see. I was the one who made that decision. But he would come to see Fedya and me every day. You know what he said to me by way of farewell? His last words were, 'Rosa, please don't wear these gum boots all the time, your legs will be aching...' Well, I didn't have anything else to wear on my feet apart from those boots.'

The rain was abating like a child tired of crying, to whom nobody had paid attention. But at the same time, behind the wall, at their neighbours', Lisa's furious sobbing started after some distinct slaps bestowed on bare flesh.

'He must have been tall and handsome,' said Innokenty in what did not sound like his normal voice.

Rosa replied that no, Mikhail was of average height and quite ordinary, even plain-looking. Besides, she could hardly remember his face. She had no photos left. She only remembered his eyes, the colour of overripe grapes. She put it exactly that way, "overripe grapes". And suddenly, she added, 'Same as this one's over here.'

Unwillingly, Sidelnikov turned his head and met her eyes. She was looking straight at him and what she said a couple of seconds later was for some reason addressed to him, Sidelnikov. She said quietly and firmly that her only man was still alive and she knew it for sure, even though she had not received any letters and of course now it was too late for letters anyway.

'But I can hear him every day, every single day,' Rosa repeated. 'And if he were dead, I would have felt it.'

She took the kettle that had gone cold and made for the door but at that moment Vassily Baronkin, drunk as a lord, materialised in the doorway. He uttered his usual greetings that consisted of: 'Hail, workers of labour!' He treated Rosa with respect and therefore every time he addressed her he would start with the words: 'I sure am sorry'. But at the sight of Innokenty, Vassily always had a face of someone suffering from heartburn and would defiantly shoot at him just one, always the same, brief phrase: 'Gimme a fag!' Whereupon Innokenty would every time report dutifully: 'Sorry, I do not smoke.' Obviously, this could drive anyone mad. Sidelnikov felt awkward for Innokenty and was amazed at the tolerance shown by Vassily, whom he had given the title of "Fire *Hydrent*". (Now, it is worth explaining that Sidelnikov had a habit of giving those around him new monikers of an absolutely obscure but expressive kind that he picked from Lord knows where. The notice "Fire Hydrent" was lettered in red oil paint on a wall by the kindergarten toilets. Such a name could only belong to Vassily, and to no one else. Another unclear inscription that read "Blak Proon" was noticed by him on a market stall of an Oriental vendor of dry fruit and soon became a second name of the cleaning girl, Galia Sharipovna, who had black hair and large eyes.)

Sidelnikov's kindly feelings towards Vassily had a very solid foundation. There was an occasion when, with the whole yard looking on, The Hydrent single-handedly hacked a pig to death. The pig was brought there in the sidecar of his motorcycle. He singed it with something resembling a gas-welding device and the next half of the day he spent chopping the meat and frying it in the communal kitchen. The smell that filled the flat was driving the five-year old Sidelnikov to distraction. Rosa had tried to distract him and even shamed him but he continued to wander along the empty corridor like a hungry puppy, while the festive droning of Baronkin's kith and kin was coming through from behind the kitchen door. This went on and on until suddenly, a fire-breathing Vassily tumbled out of the kitchen with a huge meaty bone in his hand. He was carrying it in front of him like a shaggy flower - and he was moving towards Rosa's room. Stumbling across the slightly dazed Sidelnikov in the corridor, he handled the souvenir to the boy saying, 'Five minutes gone - the flight's normal!' What followed needs no description. Happy beyond measure, Sidelnikov did not want to part with the bone even after he had polished it clean. He took it to bed with him, but already before the daybreak the precious gift perished in the rubbish bin.

...

Having heard Innokenty's usual declaration on the subject of "sorry, I do not smoke", Vassily finally could not contain his righteous fury and posed some new questions, 'Why is it that you, scum, still don't smoke? You sick or what? Or maybe you ain't no bloke, ay?' Innokenty did not have the time to answer anything because Rosa interfered and, without letting go of her kettle, said to Vassily a lot of unpleasant words, mostly along the lines of "it is you who are not a real man" and "get out of here, now!"

(It's possible that Sidelnikov would have simply forgotten this insignificant squabble, had it not become firmly tied up in his memory with what happened two months later. A grey wintry day would be drawing to a close when Tatyana Baronkin, her eyes white and staring, would walk unsteadily into Rosa's room and take a crumpled piece of paper out of her sleeve. Rosa would be silent for a long while, peering at the merciless scribble, and then, in half-whisper, would say the almost inconceivable words: "Asphyxiation from gastric content entering the respiratory tract". The Hydrent would die instantly at his work place - the cab of his lorry.)

Rosa closed the door behind Vassily and coming up to the totally wretched Innokenty asked gently:

'Are you all right? Why so sad? Shall we go? I'll see you home…'

And he, looking up to her with his crazy desolate eyes, decided to complain:

'Rosa, there's so little kindness… Why is there so little kindness?'

CHAPTER FIVE

Once Sidelnikov was left on his own in the room, he jumped up and started dashing around. It seemed impossible to grasp, or in some way tame, everything he had heard that day but something had to be done with it all. To start with, he rushed to the mirror and began to examine his own eyes with such interest as if he had only just acquired them. There was nothing about them that resembled grapes. However, their colour was undoubtedly dark green.

Dusk was already falling. The process of examining himself in the mirror was fascinating and quite soon it seemed to Sidelnikov that some silent stranger was looking at him from the other side of the glass. The face was getting dark against the background of bluish-white walls, as bare as they were on this side. The stranger was not just silent; it was as if he was stubbornly concealing in that silence the ultimate truth of what was barely gleaned from Rosa's words and what Sidelnikov would never dare ask about, and besides, afterwards there would be nobody to ask.

Suddenly blessed with a savage cunning, Sidelnikov attempted to perform a manoeuvre.

Namely, he began to shift his face imperceptibly to the left, to the very edge of the mirror hoping to discover a gap, or at least the tiniest chink, between this side and the other. Until the very last moment, he managed to hold the unblinking and strained stare of the stranger who was still peeking out of the moulded frame getting ready for intrusion… But every such attempt was met by a cool dry slap of the whitewashed wall on his cheek.

Damp smells of earth and old leaves were coming through the open windowpane and tinny clicks of individual tardy drops could be heard. Sidelnikov climbed onto a stool, then onto the windowsill and stuck his head out. He could not shake off the feeling that someone was watching him.

The air was so soft and delicious that he wanted to devour it in lumps. However, the vague need to be mindful was still lingering… It is possible that this duality brought to his mind the word "mildness" that felt unfamiliar and posh. Sidelnikov said it twice under his breath, as if tasting its milky sweetness with his tongue and lips. The word "mildness" distinctly resonated with another word that had recently sounded in the room as if wishing to find a pair. Getting down onto the floor, Sidelnikov nearly fell from the windowsill, he was so burdened by the effort of recollection. But as soon as he sat down on the stool and turned his face towards the table, the sound repeated itself of its own accord. "Kindness", that's what Innokenty said, "so little kindness".

The poem occurred so effortlessly and suddenly. It was as if it had always existed, and had just been waiting for an opportune moment in order to amaze its creator. And indeed, the amazement was in earnest. Sidelnikov was galloping around the room like a madman reciting his oeuvre in different ways with meaningful inflections. Here is the unabridged version of it:

> *Outside, the air smells of mildness.*
> *When you're forty, there's little kindness.*

He had never heard anything more impressive. Well, maybe not counting "There were only three of us /Left out of eighteen lads". True, there also was another song with an obscure but marvellous word "dreaminokarelia". An exotic female voice crooned, "Dreamin'o'Karelia will go on fore-e-ever" and it was clear that it meant something beautiful and sparkling and that fortunately, it was there to stay.

The triumphant author soon bridled his emotions and decided that he ought not to rest on his laurels. What he needed was a serious approach. Therefore, a twelve-page school notebook with times tables on its back cover was immediately sought out from the whatnot drawer. On the front cover, he printed in handsome letters:

> *Complete works of*
> *G. F. SIDELNIKOV*

And a little further down:

> *Volume 1.*

The figure "one" came out bold and important.

Being aware of the fact that any proper book should start if not with a preface then at least with a brief summary of the author, Sidelnikov was forced to obey this boring rule.

The author's summary required some serious deliberation. The summary was supposed to highly appraise and simply praise. But as the life ahead of him was certain to turn out glorious, he managed to find the adequate words:

"G. F. Sidelnikov is a well-known Soviet poet. And writer. He was born (crossed out). All his life (crossed out). He composed a lot of famous poems. He also composed..."

Sidelnikov had to decide urgently what else he would be composing apart from poems. He naturally would not allow himself the self-indulgence of piddly short stories, so without further ado Sidelnikov chose the large-scale genre.

"He also composed a lot of interesting novels"...

All that he had to do now was to invent a couple of titles, and the author's summary could be deemed ready. But he stumbled when it came to the titles.

By that time, Rosa had returned and switched on the light and sat down at the table opposite him with some of her papers and books. A bit later, she asked, 'What are you writing?' while leafing through a dog-eared German-Russian dictionary. When she learned that the preparation of his complete works was in process, she was silent for a minute and then asked the single question: 'Will you let me read it?'

The day was ending. It was one of those days which could be counted on the fingers of one hand and which Sidelnikov's memory managed afterwards to fish out of the whole ocean of the time spent with Rosa when she was still alive.

Frankly, a meagre catch. This happened due to, or maybe in spite of, the silly habit from the growing-up time: to run ahead and look forward, into the day after tomorrow, ignoring the untainted span of the present day, which was allotted the paltry orphaned role of a preparatory period. On such days, one is getting ready to start living, only to realise afterwards that it was what one had already been doing.

As regards the career of G. F. Sidelnikov as a writer, well, it is appropriate here to mention another, later event that G. F. himself preferred not to recall.

The truth is that at some point Sidelnikov, who had then already turned thirteen, did write a novel. That fantastic (if only in terms of its genre) work whose size amounted to two-thirds of a school notebook was created without interrupting his studies in the seventh form of secondary school, that is, directly during classes. The novel dealt with the burning issue concerning the fight of Soviet cosmonauts against space pirates in the circumstances of a supernova explosion. Its title was no humbler than "Lost in the Universe". When the first chapter was finished, Sidelnikov, with the notebook under his arm, went on the tram to the Old Town where was located the editorial office of the only city newspaper, "The South Urals Worker". An employee of the office by name of Deveryanov produced the impression of someone suffering from both idleness and the weight of cares. He devoured the contents of the notebook in one go in the author's presence and inquired indignantly, 'Where's the rest?' Sidelnikov, moved by such insatiability of his reader, hastened to calm him down saying, 'please don't worry, just publish it and put "to be continued" at the end, 'cause I know what's going to happen afterwards and will write the rest.' 'No way,' Deveryanov said sulkily, lowering his head, 'nothing doing.' It's clear that Sidelnikov has put a lot of effort into his work but this is not the way things are done here. First, let Sidelnikov write everything to the end, and then we'll see.

Deveryanov got this opportunity in about three weeks when he was presented with the finished manuscript, yet he requested a week for consideration. When the week was up, he laid down an unexpected condition: there are young people in the novel (he started counting on his fingers), there's a woman and a girl, but it totally lacks humour and romance. 'These ought to be inserted,' Deveryanov added kindly but firmly, thereby creating an unforeseen problem for the author. There was no problem with humour and romance. Both were effortlessly composed in the tram on the way back. But Deveryanov said that they were "to be inserted". Alas, Sidelnikov had not yet mastered the technique of insertion. Writer's work turned out arduous and grubby. Until late at night, he had to cut out intricate pieces of paper with minuscule inscriptions and paste them into the intended spaces, not to mention the fact that he knocked down the jar with paper glue twice, spilling the contents on himself. But the worst of it was that Sidelnikov ceased to understand why on earth he had bothered to go to the editorial office. He was no longer interested in what he had written. He did not feel like boasting to anyone. The grey sheets of "The South Urals Worker" used, inter alia, for wrapping a change of shoes for school, did not evoke in him any warm feelings whatsoever. Nonetheless, the notebook swollen from all the insertions was surrendered to the mercy of Deveryanov, irrevocably so, in exchange for some vague promises, but without any specific dates. Coming back from the Old Town on the same number four tram, Sidelnikov no longer remembered any supernovae and pirates accompanying them because he was absorbed in a much more crucial topic, namely, the mortal combat of Roman gladiators that he was going to depict without fail by means of linocut, and his most urgent creative task was to obtain a suitable piece of lino.

At least four months had passed when he discovered in the shopping bag belonging to Rosa, who was meeting him after school, along with the parcel with his favourite meat pies, ten identical copies of the newspaper which he did not even bother to glance at. 'You've been published,' said Rosa opening her bag.

On that day, coming out of the school building, Sidelnikov, perhaps for the very first time, took a detached view of Rosa. She was standing by the gilded Lenin's bust like a frozen sentry, in her aged threadbare brown overcoat and an old-woman's headscarf of the same brown colour and zipped cloth boots, with her bluish-black shopping bag, the only one she'd ever had, containing the still warm pies for Sidelnikov and the ten pathetic grey little newspapers.

For whom did she buy so many of them and what for? They must not be given or shown to anyone, let alone be read. Sure, he opened one of them when he was left alone with his shame and even made an attempt at playing, for his own sake, the role of an inveterate newspaper reader. All right the-e-n-n, let's see if there's anything interesting today… The headlines were intriguing and enticing: "The Union of Hammer and Sickle Strengthens", "The Targets Are Set: Let's Reach Them!", "Tradition In Reliable Hands", "Y. Shitsky: Educator And Mentor". A-ha, here we go: "Lost in the Universe". Let's see what it's about… "*It was the last hour of the night…*" Suddenly, Sidelnikov felt as if he lost the use of his arms and legs. Apart from this first phrase, everything was written by somebody else. An anonymous author, someone much more experienced, was able to conceive such exquisite expressions as "the starry expanse", "unexplored space" and "the crew's indissoluble friendship", which would have never occurred to the unsophisticated Sidelnikov.

During the following three days, the mother of the fledgling fantasy writer was receiving telephone congratulations from friends and acquaintances. Unfamiliar coquetry was bubbling in her voice. (His father was not around because it was already a year since he had left them.) Thank God, all that soon ended, evaporated almost without a trace. And in the residue, which could not be helped, there was Rosa standing in the wind in the schoolyard with the unwanted offering at the ready. It is not that Sidelnikov was ashamed of her presence, but it burdened him, ever so slightly. Besides, his enemies and tormentors could walk out of the school doors any minute and they should not be afforded any reason for sneering. Rosa seemed to have realised something and hastened her step and they walked off but not side by side. She was walking a bit ahead of him and he trudged behind, swallowing his meat pie on the go and trying not to touch with his eyes the worn out brown coat on her back.

CHAPTER SIX

She died suddenly, without burdening anyone either with her falling ill with an abrupt aggressive cancer, or with her very death. Everyone was busy getting on with their own lives. Sidelnikov's father went out to the East in search of a destiny less tangible than that of a chief electrician of the Nickel Industrial Complex and from time to time he sent letters with diligent descriptions of the Siberian weather. The mother was engaged in a continuous battle with her boss, the headmistress of a night school. After coming home from work, she would immediately rush to the phone. 'You are gravely mistaken, Natalya Andreyevna!' And a little bit later, on the phone again: 'Believe it or not, but that is what I told her, plainly: "You are gravely mistaken!"' As to Sidelnikov, he had just begun to come to his senses after his first love, which was naturally the biggest and saddest, but to be more precise, an enormous and happy one.

The beginning of his parting from Rosa coincided with the beginning of the immensely long servitude that was hiding under the innocent facade of a "secondary school". First of all, he acquired a hump in the form of a hefty satchel with rugged angles and seams that would not let him straighten his back and made him walk half-bending, lurching forward as if eternally bowing to everybody he met on the way. And very soon afterwards, with the way he walked, Sidelnikov started to resemble the smallest of the Volga River barge haulers in Repin's famous painting. He would constantly bump into those around him with the insensitive growth on his back, for instance on the tram or in the narrow school corridor, and those around him would push him back with understandable exasperation. As a consequence Sidelnikov even got used to feeling others' irritation upon his person.

Everything would have been all right, had it not gone beyond the satchel thing. At school, albeit "secondary", one had to obtain some knowledge. The first bit of knowledge garnered by Sidelnikov from the school proved to him quite excruciating. For example, he learnt that various people, boys and girls each likeable on their own, change abruptly when gathered in a pack, become somehow identical and definitely worse than they really are. In addition, whatever they are doing, they are always on the lookout, their eyes and ears searching for the person whom they have chosen as their superior, whom they are a bit afraid of and want to be liked by and whom they would like to imitate. Once or twice, Sidelnikov even caught himself giggling at the stuttering Semyonov when the latter was teased ("ke-ke-ke") by Vova Bartaev, the strongest person in the class. However, it was not just teasing people that Vova liked; he also liked to hit them in the teeth. Sidelnikov probably remembered those occasions for longer than the bashed stutterer himself.

Sidelnikov never aspired to become "superior" because to do that, one had to impose on others one's own person and whims and inevitably humiliate them. He had to make desperate efforts in order not to end up amongst the giggling or the humiliated. But there simply was no other option. Therefore, another school-born truth was that he was now on his own and nobody would help him. This was the second thing.

And thirdly, in order to assert his dubious neutrality, he had to have regular fights. The fights normally could be summed up as follows. The hesitant Sidelnikov, after a punch in the face, would suddenly fly into a rage and start to pummel at the enemy (usually the leader's sidekick) blindly and at random, until the latter gave up. Such a result of the match produced a most favourable impression upon his classmates, but Sidelnikov never reaped the fruits of his victory. Forgetting the infamous satchel or his hat, he would go home in order to cry secretly into his pillow, choking, swallowing the salty filthy taste of the fight. He would lie comatose for a few hours and then, having recovered, would firmly tell his mother that he would not go back to school on the following morning or indeed ever again. Failing to get any explanation out of him, his mother would finally transfer him to another school, where he would try to make a fresh start. But in the new class, there would always be a Vova Bartaev and after some time, history would repeat itself. All in all, by the time he received his school-leaving certificate, or so-called "Certificate of Maturity", with all the highest marks, the reasonably matured Sidelnikov had managed to pass through four different schools.

When he became a senior pupil, he would turn up at Rosa's on Saturdays, to stay overnight, and all he wanted was to get enough sleep and silence. Unlike his mother, Rosa did not ask personal questions. He would tell her things of his own accord if he felt like it. Sidelnikov was as happy and calm here as he used to be in his early days but he had already been uprooted from that life and it lost its essence.

By the time of his acquaintance with Lora, he had been in a painful and protracted conflict with his mother, the reason for which he could not recall for the life of him. Existence of the conflict manifested itself when his mother was in a foul mood, by loud addresses to "brat" and "scoundrel". When in a merry disposition, she would say, 'Well, you seem almost human!'

Sidelnikov came to the government building that was occupied by the city authorities on his mother's errand to borrow a few fashion magazines from her acquaintance, who had promised to lend them. The office was noisy with the snapping of typewriters and smelled of perfume, new parquet floors and, for some reason, of plums. The owner of the magazines was having a hasty cup of tea behind a half-open door with the sign "Department of Culture". A piece of fruitcake concealed in her cheek did not allow her to ask him strictly and clearly, 'Whom would you like to see?' It came out as 'Whod'yelikesee?' But of his awkward answer, 'I think it's you', only a croaky 's'you' remained audible. What did he manage to make out? Almost nothing, save for the girlish long legs peeking from under the desk, on her lips pink lipstick half-eaten with the cake, and short-sighted, unexpectedly old, eyes. Her name was Lora. For the whole week after this meeting, he cursed himself for having left too quickly and refusing the tea she had offered. Every now and then, he bit back his tongue in order to stop himself from inquiring whether it was time to return the magazines. And he kept holding the tattered rags to his face trying to revive the intricate bouquet of scents: the fresh parquet floor, plums and the perfume whose name he would never learn.

In exactly one week's time, they bumped into each other on the tram stop of Gagarin Square. That is, she was first to spot Sidelnikov as he came stooping to the tram stop. She recognised him and called his name. He was not surprised by the encounter and forgot to say hello because during the days that had passed he felt as if he had never parted from her. Taught as a bowstring, he was standing a couple of metres from her and did not know where to start. Fortunately, the month of September in the year in question happened to be shockingly cold and naturally, that just had to be discussed however briefly, but better still, in detail. Yet she suddenly changed the subject and confessed anxiously that in the morning, she made an exceptionally good borsch, which there was nobody even to appreciate, let alone eat. Thus, the primary love experience of Sidelnikov revealed what "happiness in private life" is meant to be. It is when the woman of your dreams invites you to taste a beetroot soup of her own making.

...

She was not that young – twenty-nine. For six and half years she had been seeing one Mekhrin, a taciturn and extremely married man, who visited her without fail on Thursdays only and clearly intended to continue to do so into a ripe old age. Every time, in his breast pocket he would bring with him a small paper packet from the chemist priced at two kopecks. The bag had an inscription "Item No.2" in the colour of manganese solution. Usually within about twenty minutes, his visit's agenda would have been exhausted. Mekhrin's taciturnity was of a universal nature and forced those socialising with him to fuss involuntarily, thus proving the law of the moral superiority of immobile objects over the mobile. Occasionally, however, he opened his mouth in order, shall we say, to notify Lora what a parasite his wife was. He called his wife by her maiden surname, Salova.

At first Lora felt shy and nervous, and then became completely perplexed. Then she would cry after he'd left. Later still, she would cry more and once she told him to go to hell with his small paper bags. But he soon came to visit again, as if nothing had happened, and she was even glad because she could not make herself become completely indifferent towards Mekhrin. Besides, better him than nobody at all. An arid time arrived, with no tears, something akin to desiccation of the soul.

Sidelnikov came to her like a bolt from the blue, like an irrepressible June shower, like a confusing squall of the elements, and she realised almost immediately that she did not wish to and would not resist this incursion. Having got used to dealing with the dreary expectation of inevitabilities, she sensed for the first time that such expectation might turn out sweet and cause a flutter in her stomach similar to the flapping of a butterfly.

Incidentally, whatever it was that she realised, was not at all obvious to him. And, if on the one side of the emerged equation there was Inevitability by the name of Sidelnikov, all feasting and adoring eyes, then on the other side there was a complete Impossibility by the name of Lora living her own grown-up clandestine life.

He did not have any right to anything because he was always dressed in the same bottle green trousers, too tight and short, that his mother had bought him two years previously when he was still in the eighth form; because he was a brat and a scoundrel; because he was ashamed of himself before this long-legged lady. One may ask, what could he hope for? But mercifully, he did not hope for anything, when, inspired by two bowls of "happiness in private life", on the next day he sold a few of his favourite books to a second-hand bookshop. For four mornings this availed him of the opportunity to buy, from obliging old ladies, sombre roses which he did not dare to give directly to the person intended; instead he furtively shoved them into Lora's mailbox, scratching his hands to bits in the process.

During those days, when Sidelnikov, like a chicken about to lay an egg, was hanging around town with the roses, half-dead from fear, gradually narrowing the circles in inevitable proximity to the single address that existed for him in the whole world, Lora made some drastic changes at home, even without quite knowing why.

On Wednesday, upon coming home from work, she called her closest neighbour, Darya Konstantinovna, in order to inquire whether Darya's husband, Nikolaich, was on the wagon at the time. It turned out that, already for the second day running, he was in excellent control of himself. In half an hour, Nikolaich, sober as a judge, and Pyotr, his inveterate domino partner, carried the old but sturdy sofa out of Lora's flat, carefully took it down to the ground floor and, as per the instruction, delivered it to the rubbish heap.

Thursday night, the immutable Mekhrin came to visit, clearly in a great haste. Failing to find the requisite piece of furniture in the appropriate place, at first his face showed bewilderment and thereupon, displeasure. He heard in reply that it was over, definitely and ultimately. Moreover, he was not to come and visit her home anymore, or else there might be consequences. Surely, he must understand. Mekhrin, who did not understand anything, nodded meaningfully, uttered 'well, well,' and departed. He was worried by the hint to "consequences", the worst of which would be publicity, insufferable in view of his status as a family man and, most importantly, of his official position. But he was not going to part lightly with something of which he came into possession long ago and to give it away to God knows whom. No later than the previous evening, sharing a bottle of cognac with a friend, albeit his junior in the office, he suddenly got all soppy and poured his heart out, boasting what first-rate breasts his mistress had. As well as the rest… So he did value Lora. But for the moment, it would be best to abstain from home visits, until such time as the circumstances had been clarified. For that, he could call on her at work, maybe even tomorrow during lunchtime.

On the next day, he entered Lora's office with the same pleasurable sensation that he always had when visiting her throughout these years, driving up in his Lada every Thursday (the day of political training, according to his cover story for the family). He felt as if every time, he was presenting a valuable gift to this slightly odd and impractical woman whom he considered a loser. Mekhrin did not show off in front of her, yet he still was very pleased with his own conduct. When being with her, he would hold his head so as to be seen in profile; no fuss, not a single unnecessary word (women seem to like that). Likewise on this occasion, he walked in, silently pushed the chair closer, sat himself down snugly and placed his hat on the desk. Looking in front of himself towards the window, he waited a little in order to give Lora a chance to appreciate the very fact of his visit, to get a bit nervous (women can't help that), and find the words for an explanation.

Indeed, she was nervous and tortured her handkerchief but, for some reason, did not wish to explain herself. She just repeated the words, 'It's over' and added dryly, 'Please leave.' Mekhrin, who knew what women's tantrums were worth, chose not to have heard. Yet somehow something felt wrong. Besides, there was a knock at the door, and a youth of sixteen or seventeen walked in. He was in need of a haircut and was dressed in a nylon jacket and khaki trousers, which were a bit too short for him. Some punk, Mekhrin registered. Yet, judging by his face, bright and cultured... The visitor uttered a shy hello and immediately headed off to the window where he found himself a place and leaned on the windowsill in the pose of one patiently waiting. Mekhrin had to turn his head away from the window and to the desk and say something for the sake of decorum. 'Well… So that's how it is. And what now?' This time it was she who appeared not to have heard. Her handkerchief was in a critical condition.

As for Sidelnikov, the stranger in the chair reminded him of a stony crag. Sidelnikov longed for him to leave as soon as possible. But with a stony crag, one might have to wait forever. And he wondered what sort of event could shift it.

In a barely audible hollow voice, Lora once again asked Mekhrin to leave. She looked terribly pretty but resembled a reprimanded schoolgirl.

Mekhrin did not as much as stir.

'Sir,' said Sidelnikov, the cultured boy, 'you have been asked to leave the premises.'

He had an ingenious idea: if an object is too heavy to lift, it could be taken away piece by piece.

'Who on Earth is that scum over there?' Mekhrin slowly asked, addressing the desk.

Next moment, Sidelnikov experienced a breathtaking sensation of weightlessness when, upon pushing himself off the windowsill he glided to the desk, pinched Mekhrin's hat with two fingers, soared up back to the opening in the window and set his trophy free. While the hat, like a fat jackdaw, was swishing obliquely through the layers of air four storeys deep and was landing on the tarmac bank of a neat little puddle, Mekhrin had the time to jump up, make a few chaotic petty movements and rush out without saying a word.

Sidelnikov was priming himself for a harder test than the expulsion of the crag.

'Perhaps you would consent,' he started, 'to go with me if, supposing… On Saturday. Because I've already got the tickets. It is just that today, I was passing by…'

She was looking up at Sidelnikov with a long gaze, that precious gaze, which would remain in his life as one of the greatest generosities that he had lived through and lost forever. But at that moment, her gaze is still lingering, and the bluish-grey icy irises hiding invisible heat begin to melt and resort to the cover of a subtle shade behind the eyelashes. Already, it started to seem to Sidelnikov that his tongue-tied invitation to see a famous French film of a love story was either a vulgarity or childish prattle. He would be put in his place any moment now and then he would have to do something about the bitter sandpaper in his mouth.

But she said, 'I would go with you anywhere you like.'

CHAPTER SEVEN

On the Saturday night, they forgot all about the cinema tickets because the two of them sitting at home in the kitchen was a fate just as enviable as sitting in the dark auditorium. It turned out that it was possible, without waiting for any reason or permission, to drink, between the two of them, a bottle of wine with the manly name of Riesling. (For want of a corkscrew, the cork was pushed inside.)

It turned out that getting ravenously hungry at that time of night was not anything out of the ordinary for either and it was all right to fry a whole pan of potatoes precisely by midnight in order to polish it off together.

For no apparent reason, it was appropriate to get into a bathtub together and wash each other from head to toe, without feeling self-conscious about kissing, or soaping with four hands at once all that was dizzyingly feminine and exaggeratedly masculine. 'Here, listen…' Sidelnikov would start, or rather, continue a thousand-and-first kitchen conversation. 'The Department of Culture is listening,' she would reply shaking water out of her ear. And at that moment, nothing seemed funnier to both than the combination of words "the Department of Culture". It turned out that it was late, half past one, and the trams would have packed up for the night – but that he could stay. (Elated, Sidelnikov recalled that it was a Saturday and that meant he was not expected at home, supposedly staying overnight at Rosa's).

All of a sudden, they fell silent, both at once. She was laying out something warm on the floor whereas he, with his forehead burning the windowpane, was trying if not to muffle, than at least to slow down the booming beats inside his left ribs. Lora said, 'Don't stand there, you'll catch your death,' and turned off the lights. Making four long steps into the darkness, he nearly trod on the pillows of the bed he was to share with her. And when, after gentle discomforts caused by noses and chins, kneecaps and feet, they managed at last to embrace one another in such a match that it seemed that their clinch could not be closer or more precise, then very slowly she opened yet another embrace, hot and terrifying like a wound that came apart. It turned out that he was able to become a boat, light yet powerful, which was speeding in the narrow riverbed, rocking the pitch darkness where an inadvertent cry and the glow of some wild lightning forestalled a quake of almost astronomical proportions.

Before they fell asleep, when it was nearly morning, Lora for some reason confessed that it was the first time in her life that she was spending a night with a man. Yet Sidelnikov did not understand straightaway that she was referring to him in such a fashion and even asked, rather stupidly, 'With whom?' She was also whispering, hiding her face in the little hollow at his collarbone, that someone handsome and strong made a gift of himself and made a certain foolish woman happy. The woman with a misty tear-stained face was sitting on the conductor's seat in the second car of the very first tram and he, ticketless, could not come up to her and pay her the three kopecks for a ticket because he was stark naked, and the covers all got twisted towards their feet, and his shoulder, to which the sleeping Lora had taken fancy, had gone numb.

The Sunday's Sidelnikov was noticeably different from the Saturday's one. For instance, he instantly became a few centimetres taller. He discovered this in the morning when, running down the stairs, he peeked into the opening of the flower box, that is, the mailbox, which had been a bit too high for him to look into even yesterday. (This iron messenger suddenly became redundant. Events of the past night gave Sidelnikov some hope for the lifelong right to give Lora flowers in person.) This precipitous augmentation of Sidelnikov's person might have been, from the point of view of Dr Pavlov the physiologist, the consequence of straightening his posture which in turn, from our non-scientific point of view, was caused, let us say, by his internal unbending. As to Sidelnikov himself, he did not bother to look for the cause and believed with confidence that a sublime promise that had always been floating in the air was now beginning to come true. It could not be an illusion. He attained the feeling of belonging, of being admitted to the secret innermost chambers, where, essentially, everything that's most important was being determined.

Furthermore, he felt unconquerable pity for the passers-by who somehow managed to exist through their weekdays, high days and holidays without possessing what Sidelnikov had. Could even a single one of these blokes standing in the endless queue for beer have been kissed on the lips when leaving home and told, 'Come back soon, I'll miss you'? In short, he felt genuine pity towards every man who had no Lora, and every woman who was not at least a little bit like her.

What was bound to happen after two months of daily dates and weekly nights spent allegedly at Rosa's, happened at last. One evening, from a payphone, the worried Rosa rang her daughter-in-law, with whom she had very little contact, and inquired why Sidelnikov had not been showing his face for such a long time.

Her daughter-in-law started, in a pedagogical voice, 'What is it, aren't weekends enough for you?' but suddenly stopped short. It was a Saturday and Sidelnikov was appropriately absent.

...

It was as if by the way and spontaneously, maybe even too much so, that his mother told him to drop by on Aunt Valya Shevtsova. Aunty Valya asked you to drop by. You ought to drop by.

Snow fell early, even before the November holidays. It was being speedily removed from Lenin Prospect by being swept away to the curbs as something alien to the forthcoming demonstration of toiling masses. Shevtsova lived within five minutes of a light-hearted walk. On the way, Sidelnikov was calling to mind his parents' talking of the legendary youth of the lady inspector who, as rumour had it, single-handedly conquered gangs of bandits. The stench of cat piss and the darkness in the entrance provoked conspiratorial fantasies. He felt like raising his collar and shoving his hands into his pockets.

Shevtsova with scanty permed hair, dressed in a flannel housecoat materialised behind the door chain.

'Take your coat off and go into the room. I won't be a moment.'

The room was dominated by an orange lampshade looming over the dining table. Plastic carnations were blooming on the mirrored dressing-table. A man's heavy snoring persisted in the next room.

'Sit yourself down.'

Shevtsova had already donned a police tunic with all the buttons done up but underneath it, her maroon housecoat was puckering in her sleeves and on her chest. She sat down across from him at the table and cast a look that hit Sidelnikov straight on the bridge of his nose. Then she said,

'It came to our knowledge – '

At the same moment, the snoring next door stopped abruptly. Someone's animal-like voice said with reproach, 'Val'ka, you stinking… bitch!' Shevtsova's face went blotchy.

Sidelnikov presumed that it was one of the bandits that she caught and gave shelter to in her home for corrective purposes.

'It came to our knowledge that you … Taking advantage of the trust…'

'I say, Val'ka, cut this crap!'

Evidently, the correction was making a slow progress.

'Anton,' shouted Shevtsova, 'will you stop it at once!'… 'That you have repeatedly spent the night away from home.'

Sidelnikov kept silent.

'We must needs know where you have been. Who you was with. And what you was doing together. Don't even dream of lying, we will find out anyways.'

Sidelnikov kept silent. The snoring next door recommenced.

She sighed and started to speak in a softer tone.

'You see, you don't realise what importance the teenager problem plays at this present moment…'

Bored, Sidelnikov was peering into the looking glass that reflected her round back and a small bald patch amongst her meagre curls.

'You see, at present, a lot of teenagers smoke and indulge in disgraceful goings-on. And some of them even engage in dirty relationships. Might it be,' she raised her voice, 'that you have been with a woman?'

Sidelnikov lowered his eyes and started to free his fingers which had become entangled in the tablecloth fringe.

'Ah-ha, that's it, isn't it!' suddenly, Shevtsova was pleased. 'Now, you're going to tell me her name. And her surname. And what you two was doing together.'

Shevtsova was practically beaming.

'And if you clam up, we'll find her ourselves. And summon her to the proper quarter. Tell the truth.'

Straining, Sidelnikov took his eyes from under the table and uttered his ultimate truth:

'Our relationship is not dirty.'

Whatever appeared in her face was greater than disappointment. She looked as if in front of her was a wretched cripple and a complete imbecile into the bargain, who did not even suspect how greatly he was stinted by Nature.

However, the "lady inspector" still had some hope left. No longer soliciting the name out of him, she asked him a question that sounded like a swansong:

'But you have a romance with her? Tell me honestly, is it a romance?'

He fell into a conscientious deliberation, in particular concerning characteristics of the genre. It was not the easiest of questions.

'No,' said Sidelnikov at last, 'I think it is plain fiction.'

A minute later, he hastily departed from the place, leaving behind a monstrous knot in the tablecloth fringe, the lampshade hit by his head rocking as if at sea, and a bitterly disappointed woman, who hated her own life for the reason of years-long absence of what she called "a dirty relationship".

CHAPTER EIGHT

Through images of that autumn and the premature onset of winter, there showed a haphazardly primed canvas onto which the autumn and winter were superimposed in a slapdash manner. Almost every event was a brutal reminder of the simple underlying reason: if an image, that is, something unquestionably visible, lives according to its own flourishing laws, with chiaroscuro, curves and creases at the lips, then so does a canvas also according to its own, with the inevitable creeping decay of the linen hessian, and nothing can be done about it.

The incident with the phone book became the beginning of pure misery and would be a reminder of itself for a long time, like a chronic ankle sprain distorting one's gait. Even though nothing much happened, really. There was a new sofa purchased in lieu of the one perished at the rubbish heap. There was, sitting on the sofa immersed in the telephone book, a taciturn beauty, whom Sidelnikov did not recognise as yesterday's Lora. It cannot be said that she was all that absorbed in the book; yet she was leafing through it with great attention, sometimes revisiting the pages she had already gone through, but this did not prevent her from picking blindly some cornflakes from a bowl and nibbling on them with the air of a preoccupied little squirrel. She was wearing a light-blue smock no longer than a man's shirt. Her bare right leg was hidden underneath her and the left one, just as bare, was set free as an independent being, all of it, from her almost childlike toes to the chamois hollow in the groin.

This inane reading went on for so long that Sidelnikov started to feel physically the diminishing of time. Meanwhile, he managed inadvertently to repair the switch in the hall, to have a sit-down on the sofa next to her, to breathe savagely down her neck, to give a stroke to her leg - the liberated one, and at the same time to ascertain her inevitable transition from letter "r" to letter "s": Savelyev, Savitskaya, Savkin, God, how many more of them!

He sat down opposite Lora mirroring her pose and unfolded a fresh issue of "The Literary Gazette". He held it in front of himself upside down for several minutes, then warily asked her if anything had happened. The answer from the sofa was a vague shrug of the shoulder.

He tried to read the editorial, for a long time staring with exasperation at the word MSILAER in its heading but, having succumbed to the unbearable angst, discarded the paper. As he asked her the question, he knew in advance that there would be no answer.

'What happened?'

He was offered some cornflakes to nibble.

He went out of the room and for an infinitely long time was roaming the dark corridor to the kitchen and back and then froze at the door jamb, staring at her fixedly. She had just leafed back through about thirty pages and then continued her perusal. He felt like throwing himself to her precious knees begging forgiveness for all his non-existent sins but was stopped by the feeling that he had witnessed a scene like this somewhere before.

'Maybe I'd better leave?' Sidelnikov asked in whisper, squeamish of his own voice and hoping that she would not hear. But she did hear and shrugged her shoulder again, this time in an absolutely clear way.

And now he was not just driven but dragged away, into the December gloom. He was kicking himself out, down five steps at a time, through the snowdrifts, and the empty sleeve of his half-pulled on coat was slapping him on the back. When he turned his head he saw that there was no light in all the windows on the third floor.

The following day, he woke up a minute before the telephone call. The morning was no different from the night before: there was the same indigo darkness in the window, and the same feeling of an irreparable loss. Normally it would have been his mother, calling to check whether he had started with his homework. In fact, he managed to do most of his homework during the breaks at school.

The receiver felt glacial. An unknown male voice asked irritably,

'Is a Rosa Sidelnikov related to you?'

'Yes,' said Sidelnikov hoarsely.

'Well then, come and collect her. There's no point operating on her. She'll have to rest at home. We have no beds left.'

'Where is she?' Sidelnikov yelled.

'Where? Hello! She's in the Chkalov hospital, the surgery ward.'

His mother phoned straight afterwards.

'Why was the phone engaged?'

He told her of the phone call. When he finished, his mother asked:

'Have you got a lot of homework to do?'

'A lot,' Sidelnikov said and put the phone down.

He ran to the Chkalov hospital through the deserted "Park of Culture and Leisure" where all the trees had frozen with their eyes closed. MSILAER, a horrid word of an incomprehensible origin was gaping in his mind. It was only when he reached the porch of the hospital building that this slippery monster turned back to front to become more comprehensible, though no less loathsome.

In the doctor's room, a weary fellow in a white hat that made him look like a chef probed Sidelnikov all over with his condoling eyes, endured Sidelnikov's breathlessly uttered questions, and with an all too obvious geniality assured him, 'Not to worry, it's just the age thing. How old is she?' He gave an encouraging wink: 'A dear old bat, isn't she.' 'Bat yourself,' Sidelnikov thought aloud, slamming the door.

He saw Rosa in the corridor. She was walking slowly, pressing her side to the wall and looking around uncertainly, like an orphan. At that moment, when she believed that nobody was watching her, she wore an expression as if there was nothing more reliable left in her life than the green wall and the enormous penitentiary gown without buttons that she held together across her stomach.

'Have you come for me? Are you going to take me away from here?'

'Yes, I have, yes I am,' Sidelnikov was repeating, trying to lift the tin-like rigid collar of her gown in order to cover her collarbones and the long thin neck.

'I'll just try and go to the loo. Sorry.'

When they came outside, she said:

'I'm so glad that it is you… I thought I'd never be outside again.'

He was leading her home, as if she were a little girl, just as she had in the other time led him home from the kindergarten.

Tatyana, dishevelled and barefoot, opened the door for them.

'Is that it? 'Ave they patched you up? 'Ow are you feelin'? They turned the water on yesterday. So I washed both meself and them floors! I'm on the third shift tonight.'

'And I'm on the second,' said Sidelnikov, for no reason at all.

In the kitchen, Lisa was feeding her baby boy, pushing a fat breast between his cheeks.

Rosa's room was unlocked. In the room, the Baronkin brothers were lying on the floor thrashing each other in the game of "Chapayev's draughts" which involved flicking each other's pieces from the board. From their flicks, Sidelnikov's plastic draughts were scattering from the board in all directions. In a few years' time, one of the brothers, Yuri, who experimented with self-incendiary arson and making shanks, would go to prison convicted for hooliganism to do his first, though not his last, stretch. Tolya, the other one, was wounded near Kandahar and would come home from a military hospital with non-healing boils on his legs but candidly proud of the round figure of Afghan soldiers he had personally killed. When a new, uncommonly modest expression "base contingent of Soviet troops" emerged in the official news, Sidelnikov every time imagined the *"base contingent"* personified by Tolya Baronkin.

Rosa politely shooed the brothers out and locked the door. She asked Sidelnikov to look away at the window because she needed to change. The sun was not bright but the snow-covered yard was almost blinding, reflecting the whole sky and sending a giant spot of reflected light into the room. On the pounded down patch between the snowdrifts, the red-haired Lydia was strolling to and fro clad in a chequered overcoat bought in "Detsky Mir", a children's department store. She was swinging a string bag with an empty milk bottle inside. Behind everything, one could discern a certain poignant truth, a transparent logic of losses whose count had already started. All of it bore the name of the withdrawing Lora, while the very novelty of lovelorn misfortune would not allow him to accept it completely.

Sidelnikov forgot that he had to stand by the window because Rosa had asked him. Turning round, he hurt his eyes with the sight that he was not supposed to see. He looked away the same second but his eye lens - or retina? – what is the tool used by this tearful and ruthless photographer? - had done its work. From that moment Sidelnikov could see the image even with his eyes closed, even in the next century.

Bent over as she sat on the edge of her chair, Rosa was taking off a cotton stocking. Instead of the tall silver pitchers, there were two long folds with wormholes of nipples drooping down to the hollow of her belly between the jutting out angles of the iliac crest. Beneath her remarkably smooth skin an ultimate earthly blackness was showing through all over.

...

'If she wants to, she could move in with us,' Sidelnikov's mother told him, 'at least, she won't be on her own.' That day, he swiped a half-litre jar of sugared lemons from the fridge at home. He took it to Rosa. She ate the lemons with obvious voracity, straight from the jar, fishing out the slippery crumpled segments with a tablespoon, one after another.

'Why don't you move in with us. At least you won't be on your own. And mother says the same...'

She stopped chewing and quickly swallowed. Then she announced in her usual cold voice:

'I've got a place to live.'

He tried to persuade her twice but she would not even listen. Pressing her was useless. Her unbending self-sufficiency permitted Sidelnikov to think that things might still get better. In any case, he did not believe in the hopelessness of her condition. It was he who could be in a bad way, it was he who was bent by his precious grief – but Rosa had to stay a permanent value. The only thing that changed from the very beginning of her illness was that she forbade visits to Innokenty, who in all these years had not vanished from the horizon.

More than once Sidelnikov would recall how, when coming to see Rosa during her last February, March or July, he was always in a hurry to leave because he badly needed to smoke and he was not supposed to do so in her presence.

CHAPTER NINE

He smoked "Inter" or "Stewardess", Bulgarian filter cigarettes that were elite and rare. To get them he had to go all the way to the railway station of the Old Town to the restaurant car of a stopover Moscow train. Unlike most his contemporaries who puffed out smoke, showing off in the school lavatory or somewhere behind the bushes – invariably in the company of others – Sidelnikov felt self-conscious about doing it in public, having decided for himself that smoking was a solitary occupation. And indeed, he was solitary again, even though he saw Lora almost every day.

Those were strange encounters. Coming from the dark street into her flat, they would almost immediately go to bed, as if gravely ill. That is, not really to bed, but, half-undressed, they would cover themselves with a blanket and would lie like that for quite some time, listening carefully to something, she lying on her back and he on his left side, facing her inscrutable profile. This inscrutability had suddenly become the main feature of her behaviour.

Sidelnikov could still stare untiringly at the beloved face. He could, without permission, cross the border between the woollen and the satiny, between the dry coolness and feverish moistness; he could get up and leave, or he could come back and ask her to marry him, he could be gloomy, tender or mad, or charge into her like into a conquered country – but that would change nothing. And after happy moans, she withdrew once more as if guarding a deep dark secret, as if she were reading again the wretched telephone directory, looking for a vital number hidden from everybody else.

Winter days, indistinguishable from one another, were crowding in on them more and more, as if forcing out the freezing life while making it clear that there was nowhere to go. On the most desperate evenings, his taking leave of Lora would be like this: biting his lip, almost without saying goodbye, with a running leap-and-a-half down the flight of stairs, with portentous deceleration at the exit of the block of flats and, finally, with a funereal stiltedness at the very first public phone. He did not have to look up the number! 'No,' she'd say dryly. 'No, you're wrong. This is not the case. It just seems so to you. No. I don't know what that noise is. Don't…You'd better be going home.' (By their absurdity, those questions and retorts of the caller aggravated further their already bankrupt relationship.)

All this did not prevent Sidelnikov from posing tricky questions to himself which he formulated clumsily, but honestly. For instance, "Why do women fall out of love?" As always, there was nobody to turn to for advice. The nearest source of romantic wisdom was kept by his mother behind the glass doors of the china cupboard, represented by about ten poetry books of varying degrees of shabbiness, collected according to the principle of what was available. Sidelnikov read poetry like a barbarian, searching in it for something akin to prescriptions, as if in a doctor's reference book. Yet it cannot be ruled out that the inhabitants of the china cupbboard themselves dreamt of exactly same thing. One of them, a namesake of a Prince of Wales, stuffed with someone else's curly bookmarks, warned sternly:

"...If your soul is pure, then you wouldn't

Kiss each other when it's just your fourth date

Or declare your love when it's your eighth!"

A nearby hardback by a prisoner of a Nazi camp caused compassion but did not relate to the subject. The others mainly hinted that heroism at work was the only prerequisite of legitimate love.

Taking into account everybody's deference to the notion of "short supply", Sidelnikov started to suspect that really good poems (like anything really good) could not be freely available in a shop or sit on a shelf in a china cupboard just like that. They ought to be obtained in a special way. An old lady librarian, whom he barely knew, reacted to

Sidelnikov's request with a searching look, and a day later brought him a leather-bound notebook to read. It contained poems by a woman with a beautiful and refined name who committed suicide more than thirty years ago. Her poems turned out not lady-like at all. They were robust and broad-shouldered and much more powerful than a lot of the male poets' verses taken together. The small purple letters on yellowish paper conveyed, better than any radio, the purest sound – an exceptionally distinctive voice of insatiable tenderness, loneliness and lofty life-long strife. Much later, Sidelnikov was amazed to find out that for the most part, female admirers of this poetry (which gradually came into fashion) were very successful and well-to-do damsels and ladies who clearly lacked only one thing in their life, namely, their own permanent tragedy.

The most unexpected novelty gleaned by Sidelnikov from the leather-bound notebook was himself, Sidelnikov's own persona. Apart from confirming the reality of apparently unpronounceable and half-forbidden developments of his soul, the poems even seemed to endorse them.

There was a ghost of self-interest because he was still too immersed in his love to read love poems disinterestedly. For example, if he encountered in the notebook an intrepid confession like this:

"I am so insatiable that

Everybody is fed up with me",

he would be desperate and silly enough to clutch his head cursing himself. It meant, of course, that "everybody", meaning Lora, who was everything and everybody to him, had had too much of him. And in this case, only feigned coldness could save him.

He would at once recall Pechorin, the "superfluous man", brutally crucified during literature lessons but whose behaviour Sidelnikov admired. Besides, nobody had yet called off the classic maxim, "the less we care for any woman, the easier she falls for us", also from the school curriculum. The point was, Sidelnikov did not have to worry about being "fallen for" because he had accidentally skipped that stage. And his admiration for Pechorin was rather speedily replaced by respectful boredom. Sidelnikov did not feel like imitating Pechorin because it was unbearably dull to waste his time and musings in order to merely *appear* someone.

...

Towards the spring, it became impossible to meet up the same way as before. Lora's second removed cousin from some regional town came to stay with her. With her curls and pale greenish pudginess, she reminded Sidelnikov of cauliflower. Cauliflower got herself a job at a food-processing factory and was, correspondingly, planning to enter a technical school for food processing. When seated, she had a habit of splaying out her arms and legs and wiggling her twenty plump digits all at once. At the very beginning of their acquaintance, when she and Sidelnikov were left on their own for a moment, Cauliflower asked him, simultaneously waggling both her manicured and pedicured extremities:

'What's between you and Lora? Are you *going out* together?'

'Yeah,' Sidelnikov said with disgust. 'We're going out on a limb. Me and Lora Nikolayevna.'

'Wow, you're just so cool,' Cauliflower was charmed.

During that time, he kept repeating to himself two lines of a poem that stayed with him like an obsession:

"My joyless passion has gone

Past the third watch",

believing that "third watch" meant "almost the limit" of the heart's endurance. The tricky questions remained unanswered, but he was not far from the truth when he sensed that the mechanism of events determining his fate had already been triggered somewhere behind the scenes.

Some evenings, Lora was late and Sidelnikov had to wait for her in Cauliflower's company. Recently, Cauliflower had got into the habit of undoing, as if by chance, the two top buttons of her dressing gown, at the same time observing her interlocutor with the air of a naturalist. She might just as well not have bothered undoing the buttons because her copious flab started directly below her neck. The guinea pig would gaze upon her disparagingly and go to the kitchen for a smoke. On one occasion, she strode after him with the air of a proprietor.

'Hey, why are you being so precious, like you're some virgin? Are you scared that Lora'd find out? Don't worry! Or would you rather I tell her that you've been hitting on me?'

Finishing his cigarette, Sidelnikov was pondering whether he should leave straightaway or, before leaving, bash her on the mousy curls with something like an ashtray. At this moment, there was a click of the front door lock and Cauliflower went to the hall without doing up her buttons. Lora, all icy crystals and pearls, in her fox hat that was his favourite, was looking at him in such a way that it was not clear whether she was really longing for him, or, was, on the contrary, sick with his being there. 'Go home, it's late already,' was all he ended up getting from her that evening. The rest was so hideous and pathetic that it hardly deserves being in this chronicle. Perhaps, it would be more appropriate in the "Accidents" section of a newspaper. The freezing to the public phone in an iron booth (his second home!); the unpleasant insolence masking his plea for a single tender word; the slamming down of the phone; the robbing of solitary passers-by of the sum of two kopecks exactly only to add more rude words from the booth, and a firm promise to kick the bucket that same day. ('Please stop. Get this out of your head … What?! Are you saying this to me? What a smart Alec… Well, keep in mind that women don't care for failed suicides' – 'Which women? You don't care for me anyway!'). The journey back, observed by the dark rows of windows and scarce trees, indifferent to their own squalor. And at home, creeping past his slumbering mother to the fridge where she kept imported sleeping pills, obtained with much effort. Then, the last supper of his life consisting of a glass of unsweetened tea and a handful of pills. Because it was a no-brainer that it all had gone beyond the third watch, with nowhere else to go. But to crown it all, he was forced to torture out his own death, in the next grade of darkness, in an undeterminable time of day or night, hugging the toilet bowl in spasms of uncontrollable vomiting.

CHAPTER TEN

Death was comprised of basic elements, all of them unnecessary, starting with getting up in the morning, washing oneself with cold water, et cetera. The streets looked as if they were a partitioned other world, where he had lived at some earlier point. There were only two places left in the town that hinted at the existence of another life, namely, railway stations. In order to leave, one needed a reason and a modicum of determination. One could use as a reason his mother's reminders to the effect that anybody more or less orderly, once they gained their certificate of maturity, left home to start college. However, nowadays not only the faraway orderly people but also nearby disorderly passers-by caused Sidelnikov's bewilderment: where were they going with such a purposeful air? Why? What for? And where on earth one could *go* anyway?

Sometimes, he would pick out one or another person in the street with a tense and thoughtful (in Sidelnikov's opinion) face and would follow him surreptitiously, hoping in this way to discover secret human *purposes*. Surely, almost every one of them must be participating in some concealed enviable life, camouflaged by concerned looks, the smell of perfume, or by fur coats, cardigans, even the doors to houses and flats. It could be coincidence, but every time the subjects under surveillance vanished in the crowd of shoppers. They were dissolved in the dumbfounding queues for vermicelli and tinned sprats in tomato sauce and port wine.

However, this did not mean that the "deceased" Sidelnikov was profoundly averse to shopping. In shops, one could encounter quite irresistible temptations. At the beginning of March, Rosa suddenly made him a present of an enormous amount of cash, sixty roubles! In a so-called "culture goods" store, he bought himself a locally manufactured record player.

Records of "Besa Me Mucho" and the singer Muslim Magomayev, which he unearthed in the closet at home, were soon worn out.

In the backyard of the hairdresser by the "Druzhba" Hotel, a muffled jingling of a recording studio could be heard. A certain Sloth managed it who at that time was the only possessor of American jeans in town. He pronounced the names of "Led Zeppelin" and "The Rolling Stones" with magnificent arrogance, but evoked Sidelnikov's sympathy by suddenly complaining that he would never get a pension since he was not a member of the trade union.

'So why aren't you a member?' asked warm-hearted Sidelnikov.

The studio manager sighed.

'You know… All those trade unions…' Sidelnikov fancied a noble valour in Sloth's reply.

Sloth recorded for Sidelnikov a few songs by Vladimir Vysotsky on photographic plates intended for X-rays. The record player was croaking but coped somehow. The songs endorsed despair but were sung in an utterly dependable and self-assured voice.

> *Maybe there was trouble with Fate*
> *and things were bad with Chance,*
> *and a taut string that lay on the frets*
> *had an invisible flaw.*

The volume was high enough to fill up the whole of the two-room flat he shared with his mother. His mother would knock on his door and demand that he shut up the racket. The racket would subside.

> *I am all clear as an open window*
> *and inconspicuous as linen cloth ...*

On the fourteenth day of his not seeing her, Lora came to his place herself. That is, she came to see his mother on some business, and throughout those twenty minutes of her searing closeness, Sidelnikov did not even come out of his room. From behind the door, he could hear his mother start talking about him. ... Gone off his head from doing nothing ...a couple of weeks ago swallowed a whole lot of pills... nowadays playing thieves' songs.

At that moment, a horrible guess dawned on Sidelnikov concerning Cauliflower. Lora had invited her to stay on purpose, in order to drive him away! Strange as it seemed, in this case, too, Sidelnikov turned out to be not far from the truth.

On the nineteenth day, a strange woman called Darya Konstantinovna phoned him and asked him to come in an hour's time to an address she dictated to him straight after. Somehow it did not occur to him to ask her what for. Everything was rolling along beyond his will, of its own accord like the cold March into the cold April. In an hour's time, when he found himself outside Lora's home, Sidelnikov thought that he was going insane. He could find this building with his eyes closed but did not know the precise address. Why on Earth did the caller asked him to come here? However, he found that the flat number she had given him was in the next entrance.

He rang the bell and waited out the silence. Then he rang the bell once again. Someone in oversized unsteady slippers rushed to the door and stopped dead, breathing unevenly. Then Sidelnikov realised that behind the door pressing her eyebrow to the murky peephole, his love was standing humiliated and wretched.

...

Afterwards she would confess to Sidelnikov that she had never been, and probably would not ever again be, as happy as she was with him during that past autumn. With him, even though he was just a powerless schoolboy, for the first time ever she felt chosen and protected. Then at a quarter to eight on a November morning, everything got smashed in an instant, together with the little glass shelf over her washbasin. Standing in front of the mirror, Lora caught herself seriously deliberating whether or not she should put on a bra. The thing was, Sidelnikov had read somewhere that to wear a bra was unhealthy for the breasts, so by no means must she wear one. Her personal health adviser! A doorbell rang so shrilly that, startled, she swung up her hand and the glass shelf with every one of its glass bottles was shattered into smithereens scattering all over the bathroom. Mekhrin with a heavy and solemn face was standing at the door.

'What on earth …'

'We need to talk.'

'I've no time.'

But he had already come in and undid his sheepskin coat.

She really was in a hurry and had no time to spare for sorting out the shameful past. She'd be lucky if she managed to clear away the broken glass and grab a cup of coffee… Upon watching her for some time as she rushed from the mess in the bathroom to the coffee pot boiling over onto the hob, Mekhrin appealed directly to the ceiling:

'Well, I used to think that I was dealing, like, with a *decent* woman.'

She threw the dust pan to the floor and came right up to him. Jabbing her finger at his breast pocket, she asked:

'What, have you not brought the Item number two with you today? …How dare you… Tell you what, Mekhrin, get the hell out. I've had enough. I cannot stand the sight of you any longer.'

He squeezed sideways to the coat-rack and it seemed that in five minutes from now, she would be able to breathe out with relief and forget all about him. But once all buttoned up, he uttered in a drawling voice looking past her:

'Well, watch out, you slut. You know very well where I work. I won't harm you … You'll offer me your arse yourself. But your snotty admirer – he's as good as done for. Looks like he dreams of a future … Well, he can go fuck himself. I'll arrange it for him. This is a small town. They won't take him even in the idiots' college. He'll beg to be a street sweeper … or a bog cleaner.'

After words like these, it would have been more logical to slam the door but Mekhrin closed it behind him gently, smooth as a minesweeper. And Lora was left on her own with the broken glass realising that from now on it was certain that she had not a slightest right to Sidelnikov and his future, all of which was still ahead of him but had already become marked by the plague…

Having decided that she would rather bite her tongue off than tell Sidelnikov of Mekhrin's intentions, she sentenced herself to helplessness. There was no other solution except to part with him. She was terrified to think about it but every evening that they spent together was increasing her sense of guilt as if she were hiding in herself a disease, lethal for her beloved. At the same time, she knew with certainty that if Sidelnikov left (for any reason), this would be a signal to Mekhrin that the place by her was vacant again and he was welcome to resume his "political studies" every Thursday. That was why a letter from the tiny town of Sorokinsk sent by a relative – some forty-second cousin –with a request to help her daughter enter the technical school for food processing and a somewhat cheeky hint at her half-empty living space, was interpreted by Lora as a blessing from above.

...

In Darya Konstantinovna's flat, there was an ingrained odour of somebody else's everyday life. There were velour covers shining red. On the bed, pillows adorned with lace were piled high to rival snowy mountain peaks. In this environment, even Lora seemed a bit strange to Sidelnikov. Overcoming his despondence, he attempted to find out what all this secrecy was for but, without uttering any sound, with her lips alone, Lora asked him to be silent. She was clinging and clinging to him, her eyelashes down and her face like that of someone blissfully asleep. All he had to do to get inside this dream was to shut his eyes, little by little freeing himself from the ugly March, his thick clothing, and the room in the centre of which they were standing pressing against each other. And it was inexplicable how she as his accomplice in the dream managed to bestow kisses on the whole of his body at once, from his lips down to his knees.

Afterwards, dropping the borrowed slippers onto the floor, light as a baby squirrel, she was climbing him as if he were a tree; reaching the cataclysmic heights where two breaths became one, and everything was hot and nothing was frightening anymore. Yet at that moment, he was the more lucid of the two of them. He managed to see the pink imprint of lipstick on her teeth and the sheen of sweat between her breasts, and even the pores of the satiny, slightly wilted skin. He was crazed by her closeness but more acute still was the knowledge that no possession, however complete, could ever quench the thirst caused by just looking at his beloved.

They remained standing like this in the middle of somebody else's room without encroaching upon its velour and lacy treasures. Afterwards, when they were having tea in the kitchen, Lora told him something she could not bring herself to say before and Sidelnikov was stubbornly and dully repeating his hopeless questions: 'Why? Why do I need to go? Why do I have to leave you? What happened? Why? What's wrong with your eyes, why are you crying?'

And she did not find anything better than to remind Sidelnikov of the occasion when he was retelling to her, with the unfeigned ardour of an eyewitness, "The Odyssey" by Homer which he had just finished reading.

'Do you remember, you said that the most important thing for him was to return to Ithaca? That he might have left with the only purpose to come back. Shall I be your Ithaca? Don't worry, I'm just joking. But I won't get married while you're away, don't you hope for this.'

On the following day, the winter ended to the soft accompaniment of the sudden drip of thawing snow.

CHAPTER ELEVEN

Later on, during the months before his leaving, Sidelnikov struggled to remember Rosa, to recall what she looked like and what she had been saying. To his consternation and shame, he could not recall anything. For some reason, other things would surface, like his washing the floor when nobody asked him to. It was just that visiting her he noticed the fluffy coat of dust under his feet and with the words, 'I'll be right back,' he went to the bathroom to get the mop and the bucket. It was not that he had some sort of a strong housekeeping reflex – more likely, he lacked it altogether, but the untidiness of the flat seemed to harbour an implicit threat. Yet is it worth remembering the way Rosa half-rises from her couch in embarrassment, as if caught red-handed, and he, care embodied, is crawling backwards on all fours spreading the dirt on the floor?

In the same nameless haze, there dispersed his final exams – the last school tribulation, the corn pollen scent of that July, the stuffiness of the second-class carriage and the enrolment competition at the philology department of Srednovsk University. Mother gave him ten green three-rouble notes and a squashed half-a-metre long jam roll. The roll got stale very soon, but for more than a fortnight it sustained the university applicant Sidelnikov at breakfast and supper. On the twenty-first of August, he left at the Dean's office a signed form that bound him to return on the first of September in order to go to a collective farm for onion picking. He hastily packed his bag that was lighter now, thanks to the disappearance of the jam roll, and after sixteen hours of merciless jolting, this time in a third-class carriage, he returned home.

As a present for his mother, he brought a foreign detective novel purchased from a drunkard at the railway station. For Rosa, he brought the large magnifying glass she had been in need of for a long time. She would never get to use it because two days later, at eight o'clock in the morning, her neighbour Tatyana would come into her room to find her lying prone on the floor.

Igor Sakhnovsky

It is from this day, when Sidelnikov was told on the phone the words "she's dead" and he ran to Rosa across the whole of the town, ignoring the stitch in his side and not allowing himself even a momentary wait for a tram, as if something could still depend on a extra minute and on his crazy haste – well, it is from this day that one could date the beginning of a new stage in their relationship that was ever unbreakable: a relationship before – between the living, and later – between the living and the dead.

On the corner of Lenin Prospect and Oil Workers Street, he slowed down, suddenly realising that he was not *ready*. That is, even if he did to some extent comprehend what he'd heard on the phone, for him it did not signify Rosa's disappearance. It felt as if to her changeless room, already cramped, was added a bulky and untidy thing called "death" which one had to get accustomed to. But he was not ready to see Rosa dead.

The room was empty. Only her slippers were left, placed neatly by the couch. Tatyana entered without knocking, her stride wide and imperious. A sniffling Olga followed her.

'You tell your mum I'll take care of the funeral. We'll see Rosa Valentinovna off properly. And I'll do the food, too…'

Tatyana opened Rosa's wardrobe (something Sidelnikov never, ever would have allowed himself to do) and upon rummaging in there for some time, got out a brown winter headscarf and covered the wall mirror with it.

'Well, y'know, she left 'er room to us, so…' The neighbour fell silent, waited a little either for objections or for gratitude and went out.

'She felt a bit better yesterday,' Olga said. 'Last night, she sat in the kitchen with us and had some food. And this morning we came into her room and there she was… face down on the floor.'

'But where is Rosa?' Sidelnikov asked quietly, as if just now they had been talking about somebody else.

'They took her to the morgue.'

Olga started crying.

He needed to smoke. But it was only after he pulled the window frame open, having conquered the tight latch, and took a cigarette out of the pack, that he realised with a start that he could now smoke inside because Rosa was no more.

…

A pauper's coffin covered with red sateen was placed on two stools in the middle of the yard. Rosa in a thin headscarf was lying in it, her face light and wet for some reason, as if she had just washed her face and had no time to dry it. Next to Sidelnikov his father, who flew in on the previous day, was shifting from foot to foot. Sidelnikov's mother did not come to the funeral. The women neighbours were whispering and sighing. A little way off, two unfamiliar old men dressed in dark suits were standing in silence. Innokenty, his head hanging and almost completely bald, was languishing nearby. All of a sudden, one of the old women let out a wail, a very sonorous and musical one, but nobody joined in and she became quiet all at once.

A small truck with its backboard lowered crept up in reverse. The driver and his mate deftly slid the coffin into the truck between the narrow seats and called out, 'C'mon up, somebody!' Sidelnikov got onto the truck, close to Rosa. His father got onto the truck too and sat down in the far corner. All the others went to the bus with a "Reserved" sign. The moment both vehicles slowly set off, there was a desperate shriek, 'Wait!' Somewhere from aside, from behind the house, the redhead Lydia darted out carrying a glass jar, from which a flower was sticking out, obviously just plucked from a street flowerbed. Nobody really was in any hurry but Lydia, spilling the water, was racing as if she were trying to catch the last train for refugees. Overtaking the truck, she changed over to a ceremonial pace and was marching in this fashion, like some guard of honour, at the head of the procession carrying the jar with the flower in front of herself, until the driver taxied onto dusty Magadanskaya street where the funereal speed was no longer appropriate.

It took them almost forty minutes to reach the cemetery. It was outside the town in the steppe. All this time, Rosa was looking at Sidelnikov kindly and serenely with her eyes closed. Even when the truck was jolting horribly on pits and bumps, and the coffin was bounding up to the height of sideboards and Sidelnikov had to lean forward and press down with both hands on her forearms and thin knees covered with a tatty sheet, Rosa still remained calm. He could not take his eyes off her wide dark eyelids and her youthful lips, looking as if they were about to smile.

It was hot and windy. The steppe was swaying, worn out by the heat. From the distance, the cemetery resembled a deserted gypsy camp. When they were almost there, the truck stalled. In the otherwise perfect silence, the driver swore, shielded by the raised bonnet. Everybody was silently waiting and Rosa, too, was waiting quietly. She seemed more alive and warm than Sidelnikov's father, whose apathetic grief could be confused with the expression of utter discontent...

They reached the cemetery at long last. Among the wind-polished gravestones and the meagre dry grass, Sidelnikov was struck by the crudeness of the clay hole where they were about to leave Rosa.

Here, two self-important gravediggers were in charge, shouting orders.

'Come up now!.. Say your goodbyes!.. Untie her hands... And feet, too... Turn down the sheet. That's it, shut the lid now... Now heave... Get out of the way, you old fogey...'

Filling up the grave, they took a break for a cigarette. Sidelnikov grabbed a spade and began to throw earth into the hole. Standing aside from everybody else, Innokenty was choking with silent tears.

Once the little pyramid-shaped structure with an iron star on top took its place on the unsteady hillock on the grave, everybody stood there a little longer and then walked back to the bus with the sense of a job properly done.

The women neighbours were exchanging words in relieved voices. The old men still remained prim. 'Whoever might they be?' Sidelnikov thought. 'Admirers, like Innokenty, or former colleagues? Wherever did she work? What was she, as a matter of fact?' And with the whole of his body, he made a movement to go back, like somebody who had forgotten to ask some important question of the person, from whom he had just parted in haste, or like someone who had left the house without the key… He turned back and froze, confronted by the new grave.

Afterwards, together with the men, he washed his hands, smarting from the spade, in the taut jet of water from the pump. He was smoking somebody else's cigarette and catching the hostile stares of his father who was already seated in the bus. His father had never before seen him so grown-up and smoking…

At the table with the funeral meal in Rosa's room, Tatyana was ladling noodle soup into bowls and saying to those who returned from the cemetery, 'Do come in, sit yourselves down.' And likewise, she said to Sidelnikov and his father, 'Do come in!'

Sidelnikov perched at the corner of the table on a stool brought in from elsewhere. He forced half a glass of vodka down his throat. He realised that he could not touch the soup and consequently was at a loss as to where he could put the full bowl unnoticeably out of sight. Across the table from him, his father was tackling the same problem with his glass – he just wetted his lips for the sake of appearance. Sidelnikov patiently primed himself for the meal taking a long time but before long, everybody simultaneously got up from the table, except Lydia who was asking for a second helping.

Having done with death as it should be done and given it its due, everybody was wandering off to get on with their lives. His father was flying back that night.

Oil Workers Street had by now completely forgotten about the person called Shkiryatov. After walking in silence for two blocks, his father started cheerfully:

'So you're a student now!'

'What? Oh yeah…' Sidelnikov was distracted and absolutely drunk.

'Your mum complains that you are rude to her and that you don't listen to what she's saying.'

Suddenly, Sidelnikov felt nauseous – he barely managed to dash aside to be sick behind the corner. His father was wincing and looking at his watch.

'So why can't you get on with your mum?'

'She shouldn't humiliate me,' coughed out Sidelnikov feeling like a kindergarten snitch. By the tram stop, he suddenly remembered:

'Could I go to the airport with you?'

'No need. It'll be too late for you.'

He dryly parted with his father and went straight back from the tram stop, hoping to sleep over at Rosa's for the last time. Slightly perplexed, Tatyana let him stay. The room, already tidied up, was pretending that no funeral lunch had taken place in there and that earlier, nobody had been lying there face down on the floor. Everything looked innocent, except that one of the two slippers must have been kicked under the couch in the bustle.

He could not find a bed sheet and put a blanket cover on the mattress on the iron bed. It was getting dark fast and moths began to invade the room through the window. Sidelnikov turned off the light, stripped naked and lay down, covering himself with the worn-out itchy blanket. In the darkness by the window, there immediately appeared something like a blind spot, impenetrably black. He had to half-rise in order for the blackness to take the shape of the mirror covered with the scarf.

Why was it done? He was told that something might stay in the mirror. The soul of a dead person? Or a reflection of death? If there was any reason, however feeble, in this custom, then this was the right time to check it... He came up to the mirror and yanked the scarf off. A tiny powdery body of a butterfly hit him in the face. Somebody naked and dishevelled was looking back at him wildly, his eyes glistening.

By the age of seventeen, Sidelnikov had worked out his own self-made physics, nurtured exclusively by intuition. For instance, according to his crude theory, any object, whether alive or not, should, in order to be seen, emit particles, which were fast and tenacious enough to penetrate the pupil of a spectator or the depth of a mirror. The night before last the mirror, not yet blinded by the scarf, reflected the lonely death on the floor, which meant that it might have absorbed the particles comprising the image of that death.

It did not occur to Sidelnikov to correlate his "physics" in any way with the namesake school subject, since he did not feel any academic confidence in the teacher, a retired major, who used to say when calling a pupil to the blackboard, 'C'mon now, make it snappy! Nature, it friggin' ab'ors a vacuum!'

Having adapted to the silence of the room that had lost its mistress and to the nocturnal breathing of August outside the window, Sidelnikov was trying, if not to measure, then at least to feel the dire consequences of Rosa's departure. But after lengthy and painstaking listening, when it was already about midnight, he started to realise that there was no direness at all. It was only his, Sidelnikov's, soul that was devastated by what had happened, whereas everything around him was abiding in a peace so complete, it was as if the world was a chalice that stayed intact, without the slightest depletion, or spilling of a drop, and was rather even somehow replenished.

Over the abating chorus of cicadas and murmur of the trees, and over the sleepy sighs of the town – above the whole thing – one could hear the oceanic effort of some colossal lungs that miraculously coincided in rhythm with the even breathing of Sidelnikov curled in a foetal position already almost asleep.

Before he drifted off, he remembered to screw up his eyes very tight in order to make certain that the tiny creatures visible only from the inside of his eyes, under the shut eyelids, still continued their hasty mysterious life.

They did, as if nothing had happened.

CHAPTER TWELVE

Once he got to the village, he sent Lora a letter where impatient and sad words were accompanied by a cartoon with an inscription, 'And that's what's happening to me.' The picture showed a black onion field under drizzling rain and the tiny insect-like figures of students, laden with sacks and plodding unswervingly to the gigantic goal, a tractor-pulled trailer stuck in the mud.

He waited in vain for a reply to this letter – and the two following ones.

The lady of the house where he was allocated to stay, a large doughy woman of uncertain age, was observing Sidelnikov's epistolary efforts with respect and afterwards, complaining about her broken spectacles, asked him to take down a letter on her behalf.

'How do you do my elder daughter Lyudmila and your husband Vyacheslav...' Sidelnikov was scribbling to loud dictation.

'In the first lines of me letter, please be advised that we are livin' well. Me legs are achin'. And despite that potatoes was not picked before the rain started, there's not a thing in the house and your little brother Nikolai lies on the stove and pisses his pants...'

'Don't fib, that was only once,' Nikolai, who was also present, objected limply.

"... lies on the stove and has wetted himself (once only)", inscribed Sidelnikov with the resolute hand of a seasoned editor.

The village life filled him with bleak consternation. It was not just because the rich knee-high mud was swamping everything. Sidelnikov had almost got used to having to extract his feet like hefty tree stumps with every step when walking from home to work and in the field itself. Every new step encountered new mire, now on the left, now on the right. But even when he was asleep he remembered that he would soon go away from here, whereas in the faces of the village people, especially the older ones, in their bearing and their champing gait, one could perceive a life sentence to this place which they would be ashamed not to love, since it was home.

When the sky cleared for short intervals, the onion field began to resemble a beach. The first year girls would take their sweaters off, their colourful bikinis gleaming in the sun. In the mess of the primeval dirt, the prettily undressed girls appeared even more pretty and undressed.

All of the boys without exception – there were three of them, not counting Sidelnikov, – wrote poetry that they read to each other at every opportunity until they were blue in the face. For instance, under the cover of the rattling tractor, the hippyish poet Kostya would recite an epistle to his faraway sweetheart, "Gently! You're entering me!" This phrase was repeated at least twelve times like an admonishing refrain:

Gently! You're entering me!

That is to say, please enter but do be quiet; don't make this awful noise like the tractor here...

Another poet, the bearded Yuri, unexpectedly dedicated a poem to Sidelnikov but instead of showing it to the dedicatee, circulated it around like an anonymous letter. Presumably, because the dedication contained a bitter reprimand:

Why aren't you drinking with the beardies?
Why aren't you joining in our songs?

They were in fact drinking diligently, though not very expertly. Once, Sidelnikov took part in a bash set up by Beslan, the son of a public prosecutor. (When meeting new people, he would actually introduce himself as "Beslan, the prosecutor's son".) They purchased in advance and hid the bottles of Agdam wine as if they were contraband explosives. When it grew dark, they made a bonfire by the field. The two girls invited to the party appeared to Sidelnikov extraordinarily beautiful. Efficiently, they spread a sheet of cellophane on the ground and put out the tomatoes they brought with them. All four of them were somewhat unnaturally animated but did not know what they should drink to. The prosecutor's son started every sentence with the words, 'Well, us in the mountains…' Sidelnikov kept silent. The wine allegedly made from "berries and fruit" tasted a bit bitter, like burnt sugar.

The tall girl, Natasha, was smiling at Sidelnikov mysteriously, while at the same time not forgetting to supervise the short and skinny Lyuba. She snapped to Beslan who got too ardent, 'Don't grab my silly bits!' When Lyuba put her mint-smelling head on Sidelnikov's shoulder, Natasha called her up and asked pointedly in loud whisper, 'Do you remember that it's our time of the month today?'

That night, Sidelnikov dreamt of Rosa. They had a conversation, light-hearted and about nothing in particular. But Sidelnikov was confused and scared by the scarf on her head that was on back to front completely hiding her face as if it was the back of her head. Sidelnikov asked her why she put the scarf on like this.

'It's best that you do not see me the way I look just now.'

They talked a bit more, about something insignificant, and she said, as a non-sequitur, 'On the plus side, now I know everything about you. Only please do not be scared of anything, anything at all.'

By the middle of the month, it looked like the weather had come to its senses and lightened up and strangely, at the same time the fieldwork petered out. The hefty fellow from the Komsomol committee, with his sleeves always rolled up but his hands never out of his pockets, stopped spurring and egging them on. Then the tractor broke down. A couple of times Sidelnikov was entrusted with a horse and a cart. Totally happy because of the complete mutual understanding between him and the downcast nag, he was amazed at the redundancy of the reins. Within sight of his destination, he would start mentally rehearsing the commanding intonation for the word "Whoa!" However, the trusty steed would stop of its own accord exactly when needed. On the third time, the stableman was in a bad mood and made Sidelnikov go away with nothing for his pains, grumbling something to the effect that the horse had broken down too, same as the tractor. From now on, for days on end, one was able to lie on one's back face to face with the September sky that expressed nothing except a sense of homelessness.

Closing his eyes, he would see Rosa who was at that moment lying in the same way, supine, only there was no sky above her but two metres of clay and a board covered with red sateen. However, in his dreams she was alive and smiling, but almost never speaking. By all her behaviour, she let Sidelnikov understand that really there was nothing to grieve for and everything was all right. Thus he would wake up heartened – and if somewhere in the background of a dank morning he stumbled in his memory upon the recent funeral, then the latter appeared as an incomprehensible blunder attributable to no-one.

Soon afterwards, one of the first year students had a brainwave and applied to the hefty fellow from the Komsomol committee with a private confession of dysentery symptoms. The applicant averted his eyes and shyly bit his cuticles, and was dismissed from the collective farm to the four winds. Instantly, the disease acquired the nature of a bandwagon. Sidelnikov fell the ninth victim of the epidemic.

...

In the city, the early autumn was still observing some decorum prior to collapsing face down in its own dirt. The young provincial was not interested in settling down on the few square metres surrounding his hostel bed – he was drawn to the avenues and parks at the very least. He also liked to simply stand waiting at public transport stops, where he could think of any of the approaching trams and trolleybuses as "mine" or "not mine" on equal grounds since there was not a single address in town where he would be expected. The way such addresses appeared in one's life seemed to him now a crucial mystery of nature.

Without knowing why, he would enter the hairdresser's, which labelled itself a "salon" but smelled like a combined bath-and-wash-house. Sidelnikov would secure a place in the queue, even though he was in no way intending to have a haircut. From the half-open door of the "ladies parlour", from its mirrored insides, a steamed-up young empress in a white turban looked at him haughtily. Under her throne, he could see her round foot in an opaque stocking take itself out of its high-heeled shoe and rub its small semi-transparent heel against the other foot. A courtier asked him, 'Would you tell them that I'm next in the queue after you?' 'Certainly,' Sidelnikov replied obligingly, clearly already admitted to the high society circle.

This city, founded a few years after St Petersburg, was guilty at first of a slightly daft imitation of its elder sister, the "Northern Capital". Even their names rhymed. However, over a couple of centuries, as the times grew ever more cruel, it stopped caring about any family likeness; it changed its name and, after a short stint of leftist inclinations, set off on the rocky but straight path to military and industrial classicism. The pediments of Houses of Culture accommodated a tense pile of workers, soldiers and sailors with expressions of such intimidating righteousness that, passing by under their stony gaze, Sidelnikov felt out of place and in the wrong.

On these streets, under the eye of official signboards, he started to experience something like fear of being exposed, even though he could not imagine what it was that he had to hide. For some reason, he recalled Mekhrin with alarm, although he had only met Mekhrin once and never thought of him since. It seemed to him that the whole city was under the command of hat-sporting stony crags like him. But he would find adequate comfort in two warm meat pies wrapped in greasy paper, purchased in the street and consumed in understandable proximity to the tin stall selling the delicacy in question. That was his lunch. As a rule, he forgot to have dinner.

He was lucky with the place at the hostel. Everybody else was shoved into six-bed rooms, whereas he got a two-bed one, to share with one Ghena Shtrausenko, who was the hostel watchman and looked like a shepherd and a sheep at the same time.

'So,' Shtrausenko said, with affected sternness, 'let's live *reciprocally*. I bring here whoever I want and you bring here whoever you want. When in Rome… ya know. Is it okay with you?'

Sidelnikov did not mind and steeled himself to become a live witness to wild debauchery. However, in reality the secret drama of the twenty-eight year old Shtrausenko was the complete disregard of him by girls and women who were not in any way tempted by the sheep-like appearance of the watchman and his shepherd's manners, perfected in combat with a herd of students.

At night, Sidelnikov was woken up sometimes by the strange shrill sounds produced by his roommate's bed. It seemed in the dark that Ghena was trying unsuccessfully to saw the wire springs of the bed…

When Sidelnikov started to get visits from the girls in his year (for lecture notes or a ciggie), Shtrausenko decided that he was dealing with a ladies' man and completely changed his tone.

'Right. You've loads of skirts, haven't you? Now then, pick one and arrange it for me. Got it?'

'No,' Sidelnikov replied, 'I haven't got it. I am not here to pimp for you.'

'Well then, you're not gonna last here,' summed up Shtrausenko and went off to work to keep watch.

CHAPTER THIRTEEN

Apparently, Rosa did not much need everyday memories of herself and was satisfied with Sidelnikov's dreams, which she would enter unhindered, just like that, in order to stay a little, to see him and reassure him by her presence. Gradually their roles took on shapes as if he was a paratrooper, risking his life every second on the brink of a feat or a disaster and needing special assurance, whereas she, Rosa, was completely safe and sound. Thanks to such a perspective, the anguish of murky autumn mornings on the damp icy pillow, with pains of hunger in the pit of his stomach, became more bearable.

At the university lectures, Sidelnikov sometimes imagined that he was going mad. He was overcome alternately by fits of fear or laughter. For instance, it was scary to meet the eyes of the department's authorities who could at any moment suspect Sidelnikov of not being the person he pretended to be, and throw the fraud out in the street, where he'd be able at last to identify his real self and hear himself out at leisure. Naturally, if this happened, he would not tell his mother anything, at least not until he'd got conscripted. But, while looking for a spare bench at the railway station to spend the night (since he would obviously be thrown out of the hostel, too), he'd be unlikely to regret his idiotic laughter at the Dean's lectures.

The Dean, whose surname was Kulkov and who was responsible for Russian Soviet literature, drew with chalk on the blackboard a scale of writing talents that looked like a sports champions' podium. The highest step, that of the winner, was occupied by Gorky, whereas Bunin was skulking at the very bottom, with his name unfinished because the chalk ran out.

Kulkov was very troubled by the poet Alexander Blok.

'You see,' he was saying with ardour, 'These here poems about the Fair Lady, they were, like, only compose-ed during the period before the wedding! But once our friend Alex and his bride … er…' Kulkov was looking for a better word, slowly bringing together his index fingers, '…got, so to speak, er… *coupled*, it was then that he, you understand, stopped writing them poems…'

Sidelnikov was hiding his nose in his fist risking suffocation and was coughing and sneezing at the same time. He was looking around at his fellow students, but everybody was listening with appropriate attention, and nobody was laughing.

In Sidelnikov's briefcase, there was a faint Xeroxed copy of "The Gulag Archipelago" borrowed from somebody. Without doubt, had this outrageous fact come to Kulkov's notice, Sidelnikov would have had to identify himself and hear himself out not just in the street but also in certain chambers. (Who could have foreseen the crazy times when Kulkov would embrace anti-Soviet literature into his fervent sphere of competence, by writing a whole monograph on Solzhenitsyn, which, however, would go almost unnoticed by his ungrateful contemporaries…)

They started to recognise Sidelnikov at the trunk call office where in the early days he went to phone Lora nearly every evening. He did not just walk, he hurried there like a wounded recruit to the aid station to have his dressing changed. As a preliminary, every time a complex mathematical procedure took place, in order to calculate a certain fraction where the fragile numerator, the cash in his pocket, was crumbling into nothing before his very eyes, whereas the denominator was swelling up comprising imaginary meat pies which had yet to be bought one way or another, and the minutes on the phone which never seemed sufficient to Sidelnikov. 'Hello,' he would shout, hungrily listening for her voice, 'that's me!' But Lora's reply would be always reserved. It was so cold and reserved that the precious minutes, saved with such trouble, would be enough and to spare, same as his joy. In thirty seconds, it would turn out that they had nothing to talk about. And Sidelnikov would drag himself back to the hostel hating telephone communications as such, and Cauliflower, whose presence it surely was that stopped Lora from speaking normally, and, above all, his own foolish raptures. 'Shut up! Drop dead!' he kept telling someone inside of him, some soft hatchling nestling in his solar plexus. He had to get used to the fact that the gift love once bestowed on him to keep forever, could be easily taken away without any explanation at all.

Igor Sakhnovsky

The hostel was inhabited by provincials. In the eyes of their provincial friends and relatives, they appeared the lucky ones who had made a bold leap into big, real life like the one shown on television. This real life in the hostel started late in the evening, towards the night time, when no shops were open but everyone felt like eating, drinking, smoking and socialising. They used to stroll along the narrow corridors of the five floors as if along village roads in their slippers, flowery dressing gowns and tracksuit bottoms. The worst vagrants would look into the rooms of more provident ones and would cadge, brazen as can be, a bite to eat or a smoke. Those who gathered around a blackened tea kettle or a bottle caused envy. The utterly despondent hostel's "orphans" were noticeable. They did not mix with anyone, but were happy to partake of any feast. In this respect, the shabby Shtrausenko's room represented an El Dorado because drinking went on in there nearly every evening of the week. Shtrausenko was visibly proud of the fact that his cronies kept coming to him from all over the city. However, as Sidelnikov observed, Shtrausenko's guests were just using the premises as a landing for imbibing the liquors obtained, and were suffering the presence of their host the same way they put up with the meagre morsels, like the stale processed cheese that accompanied their drink.

Amongst the hostel's "orphans", the gap-toothed Nadia stood out particularly. She naturally did not consider herself an orphan, but, on the contrary, was shamelessly resplendent like an Italian film star with attire to match. Her clothes were either very long, reaching to the floor, or very short, but always tightly fitted, spangled and baring half her chest. The absence or irregularity of some of her front teeth did not impair Nadia's beauty. However, she was usually shunned and avoided as if she were contagious or politically unreliable, possibly because for some mysterious reasons Nadia had been expelled in the fourth year and resided in the hostel illegally, like a stray cat.

Lighting her own cigarette from his, Nadia said a baffling flattering phrase to Sidelnikov.

'I will probably like you. Somehow you seem a bit Proustian.'

He became embarrassed and inadvertently fixed his gaze on her legs that made one think of thoroughbreds. Next to Nadia, he felt as if he was in the wings of a circus or in a ballerina's dressing room.

Normally, she would appear in Shtrausenko's El Dorado when the first bottle was nearly finished. She would casually drink up what was left if there was only one bottle. When there was more than one, she would at first refuse but later agree to drink and in any case drank little but stayed till the very end. Because of that, Shtrausenko called her a freeloader behind her back, but in the presence of his guests treated her as a bothersome mistress. Obviously, he was certain that it was bound to happen sooner or later – in his opinion, she was a safe bet since she kept coming and sitting there every evening. Nadia tolerated such handling with remarkable meekness or, rather, pretended not to notice it.

After the conversation about skirts and pimps, Shtrausenko stopped inviting Sidelnikov to the table. Excommunicated from the feasts, he was only happy about it because he got fed up with going to bed drunk. From then on, he used to ignore the feasts, lying on top of the blanket on his bed and reading books. When his roommate went on duty, Sidelnikov took over the unoccupied table. On such evenings, the gap-toothed Nadia would call in too, for about five minutes – to have a fag and to ask a couple of indiscreet questions. For instance, she would materialise in the doorway in an enormous halo of shining black curls, though on the day before her hair was dead straight and chestnut colour. She would whirl up the luxurious mane with both hands over her head and inquire:

'How do you like my new image?'

'Very,' Sidelnikov would give an exhaustive answer.

She looked at that moment like the Duchess of Alba from the film "Goya" which he had seen recently. With her arms raised, her armpits displayed unbelievably smooth whiteness.

'And what do you like best?' Nadia wanted him to be more specific.

'The armpits,' confessed Sidelnikov.

'You shouldn't be so indifferent, young man,' Nadia rebuked him before leaving.

'All right, I'll improve,' he muttered indistinctly.

CHAPTER FOURTEEN

This pair clambered on the tram with difficulty. They stood out among the other passengers by reason of their deliberate estrangement from everybody else – it was as if they had been forced to take out a piece of enclosed space from their meagre home and carry it along like a secret little cradle through the street and tram crowds, protecting it from collisions. This way one carries an expensive rustling bunch of flowers or a fractured arm in packed public transport – this is how the pair must have chosen to carry themselves. But in fact, they were bristling and sticking out and bumping into everything and everybody.

The two, a little boy and an old woman, squeezed through the crowd to a free seat. He sat down at once and she stood next to him. The boy was about six or seven. A brief glance at his senselessly half-open mouth, the flattened bridge of his nose and the reddish crinkles around his piglet-like little eyes was enough to recognise Down's syndrome. The old woman, who looked like a dried blade of grass, was taking a handkerchief to his face trying to wipe something off. But the boy waved her off slapping resonantly on her forearm with his chubby underdeveloped hand. Altogether, he was behaving like a Crown prince: his subjects with their lowly needs were bustling around him – they hastily packed themselves into the carriage dragging bags splattered with the autumn mud, whereas there was nothing left for him other than to gaze mournfully at the realm that was his lot and was far from perfection.

Sidelnikov, gripped by the crowd, could not take his eyes from the Down's child, amazed by the fact that in the piglet-like little face of the child, he could indeed discern an almost regal dignity or even pride. And then something self-evident dawned upon Sidelnikov: the present and the future of this boy and his protection and his realm and all his subjects were all converged in this scrawny bent old woman who could barely stay on her feet.

He got off the tram at an unknown stop, shuffled to a bush at the side of the road and halted. He forgot where he was going; he was shaken. All he wanted at that moment was Rosa. The surrounding world was made of her absence. The banished hatchling was frantically thrashing in the thicket of his solar plexus, making his whole body tremble. These signs, sickeningly shameful in his opinion, made him realise that he was sobbing. Not having dropped a hint of a tear by Rosa's coffin and grave, there he was, in this strange city, at long last mourning over her who had not lived to be loved by him.

It seemed that Rosa did not pay much attention to what had happened. She continued to visit his dreams, but would talk to him as little as when she was alive. But it also might be that by morning, he would have forgotten her words. Over three weeks, Sidelnikov recalled one phrase she repeated twice, that he'd better move to another room. However, he had become used to their two-bed hovel and felt sorry for those who had to share a room with another five people.

Guests with bottles were popping round sometimes frequently, sometimes hardly ever. The sharp aroma of Nadia's perfume practically never evaporated from the El Dorado. Once, when Shtrausenko was not there and Sidelnikov had just wiped the sticky stains off the table and spread out his notes on English, Nadia appeared before him as a short-haired blonde clad in something like a slippery night-gown.

'Is Gennady at work? That's good.'

All of sudden, she turned the key in the door and came up to Sidelnikov, walking with the relaxed gait of a model. He could smell face powder, wine and her sweetish sweat. While he was stupidly correlating the rights of a spectator with the duties of a gentleman, the show had time to begin.

He was still sitting on his chair immersed in idiotic qualms as to whether he was allowed to watch Nadia taking her shoes off and by an impatient sinuous movement hitching up the tight black satin and freeing her naked hips from under it, opening out her legs in a sort of a ballet-or-circus split and, without taking her widely spread feet off of the floor, pulling herself like a wet glove onto the hot idol which, a minute earlier, she had extracted out to the daylight and caressed hurriedly and crossly.

In his mind, Sidelnikov compared himself with a sports apparatus that came in handy for a breathtaking gymnastic exercise. Neither of them uttered a word. The rhythmical breath of the gymnast and the resonant smack of conjugating flesh provided the only soundtrack to the scene.

The rap at the door was obviously out of tune. But the knocking was imperiously loud which meant that Shtrausenko was back. The characters in the scene feigned temporary deafness. The watchman banged at the door some more, then yelled, 'Bugger!' and cleared off. In a minute, Nadia left too, saying by way of a goodbye:

'You are not going to believe it, but I like you already.'

Igor Sakhnovsky

Sidelnikov did not know what to do with himself, wet and sticking out. Sidling like a saboteur, he stole along the corridor to the shower room and got under the gushing water. His state was both delicious and nauseous.

...

On the next night, Shtrausenko was receiving his usual visitors. By half past midnight, the disposition was as follows: at the table, there were the host inspired by port, Nadia with an unfinished glass of wine, one guest blissfully sliding down off his chair into nothingness and another guest, wistful like Byron but with a wart on his brow. Sidelnikov was sitting on his bed with a newly purchased book of poetry.

The conversation was going on as follows.

Shtrausenko (archly):

'Nad'ka, d'you need cash?'

Nadia (looking into her glass):

'Yeah.'

'For how much would you put out for Sergey?'

Sergey (briefly pausing in his slide off the chair):

'How much what?'

Nadia (to Sidelnikov):

'You seem to be reading some poetry?'

The warted 'Byron' (sullenly):

'You cock teaser!'

'What kind of poetry - hope it's not a secret?'

'Er... well, it's just...'

Actually, the poetry was of the kind that made one either straighten one's breath or stop breathing altogether: "She had come into a new virginity / and was untouchable; her sex had closed / like a young flower at nightfall, and her hands / had grown so unused to marriage, that the god's / infinitely gentle touch of guidance/ hurt her, like an undesired kiss …"

Shtrausenko (theatrically):

'You sat on the lap

Of many a lad…'

Nadia:

'Please - just a few lines!'

Sidelnikov (reluctantly, in singsong)

' She was no longer that woman with blue eyes…'

Shtrausenko:

'I'm some poet, don't you know it!'

"…no longer the aromatic island in the theatre box / and that man's property no longer…"

'Keep it short!'

'Shtraus,' Nadia asked, 'shut your mouth.'

'Don't you bloody shut me up! She comes here every bloody day, gets sozzled for nothing and now she's gone all clever…'

Nadia put her glass down gingerly.

'I've never seen *you* pay for your own drink,' said Sidelnikov to Shtrausenko.

'You bloody bitch!' Byron said sullenly, to no one in particular.

'Freeloader! Go get a job. You've got some extra teeth left, shall we count them for you.'

'Is that you who's going to count?' asked Sidelnikov.

'You bloody bitch,' Byron said again and unexpectedly slapped the watchman's face. The latter ignored it.

'With sluts like you, I'd only count till two. One, two - fuck you!'

'Look at the performing sheep, it can count to two,' said Sidelnikov choking with sudden fury.

'Shall we step outside?' Shtrausenko offered, not very firmly.

But Sidelnikov had already gotten up from his bed and was putting his shoes on. He had never wanted to fight as badly as he did now. 'Let him… let him start first, I'm not going to spare him.'

They paused, biding their time in the blind gut of the corridor, vacant at night. The watchman's trick could not be simpler. Hesitating, he cast a roguish glance beyond Sidelnikov's shoulder. Sidelnikov turned to look back and a moment later got a merciless blow smashing his nose cartilage, accompanied by a high-pitched twang like that of a snapped piece of ice, and by the sultry odour of blood. Completely blinded, he thrust his fists out several times, at the treacherous air, at the invisible stubbly mug, and when he heard the tramping of Shtrausenko's running away, he sat down on the floor with his knees apart and hung down his head so that the salty red stream could trickle out unhindered.

CHAPTER FIFTEEN

The only thing that interested the militia lieutenant who stuck to Sidelnikov at the casualty ward of the City Hospital Number One, was which of the fighters was drunk and which wasn't. Sidelnikov, who had been brought in by ambulance, answered reluctantly. By the end of the interrogation, he attempted to use the "comrade major" as a looking glass in order to find out the exact location of his broken nose.

'Precisely under your left eye,' replied the raised in rank.

For the rest of the night, Sidelnikov was being sent around: from the first floor to the fourth ('Go to X-ray'), from the fourth floor to the first ('Wait downstairs') and then back to X-ray ('Go get the image'). At first, the negative was bad, the next one was good but some important card was missing, and so on, and so forth.

During yet another ascent, somewhere between the first and the fourth floors, Sidelnikov nestled his temple against the cool wooden banisters and tried to go to sleep. But then a girl in white came flying from the darkness and shouted, 'Patient, why are you walking around! You aren't allowed to walk at all!' He was knocked down onto a trolley and taken into the operating theatre. The last that he remembered of that night was a heart-to-heart conversation with the surgeon who asked him a strange question:

'Well, shall we tie you up?'

'What for?'

'It's going to hurt a lot, and there'll be no anaesthetic.'

'What are you going to do?'

'Set your nose straight.'

'No need to tie me.'

…He was put in the corridor, in everybody's way, where he woke up six hours later because the bandage on his face was soaked through with blood. The following half of the day he had to spend close on the nurse's heels humbly begging her for a new bandage, in order to replace the bloodstained muzzle with a clean one. It was as if he was rehearsing for the role of the Beast from "Beauty and the Beast", trying to woo the timorous Beauty. 'Can't you see, I'm busy,' exclaimed the maiden, running away from his monstrous deformity.

In the evening, Beslan, the prosecutor's son, paid an unexpected visit to the hospital.

'Shtraus is offering to pay you. Four hundred roubles.'

'What for?'

'He's scared that you're going to get him locked up. For example, we in the mountains…'

'Tell him to go to hell!'

On the next day, the offer rose up to fifteen hundred.

Beslan's eyes were shining.

'Just think about it – and five hundred up front!'

Sidelnikov made an attempt at a rude curse but stumbled because he forgot the order of words needed for the occasion.

'What shall I tell him? How much do you want?'

'Let him find me another room, I won't share with him anymore.'

He wrote a short letter to his mother, which took him a whole hour ("All is fine with me, I'm studying. I'm well…"). Afterwards, he lay in bed for a couple of hours, staring at the ceiling embellished with stucco mouldings and perceiving a devious connection between the ceiling's formidable extravagance and the wrongs of his own life. It was clear to Sidelnikov that at some stage his life had gone awry but, much as he tried, he was unable to detect any trace of the fault itself.

Having rested enough, he set off to explore the hospital where he was to spend more than a week. Everything in it was oppressive on account of its huge size and lack of comfort – the flights of stairs, corridors, corners and dusty plants in tubs, window openings and draft. Here, people were not living, but waiting out in pain for the gap in time to close, like in prison or at a railway station, which also could turn into a final destination. Everybody was waiting for the "rounds", "visits" and "parcels" – those were the most exciting words. Perspiring visitors were crowding the little bay on the ground floor in poses of seeing off or meeting, with plastic carriers, jars or string bags at the ready in order to shove them at a propitious moment to a random courier from amongst the departing, who were scurrying around in pyjamas and bed slippers on bare feet ('Excuse me, which floor are you from? Would you please…').

Nobody came to visit Sidelnikov. But he regularly went downstairs to the bay and peered at the faces in the crowd, pretending he was looking for someone – and would leave with parcels to take to someone else.

Igor Sakhnovsky

The hugeness of the hospital was partly concealed by a great quantity of partitions intended to hide certain unsightly contents. From behind doors, screens and sheets, from under gowns and bandages, fragments of pale nakedness and blood clots were peeping out, fusty odours and moans were escaping, breaking the sterile decorum. A red-and-black wad of cotton wool dropped by someone in the corner of a bathroom reduced the stern significance of the hospital gospel to its basic elements.

One evening before supper Sidelnikov explored a narrow passage in the recess under the staircase that he had never noticed before. Behind the inconspicuous door, a low, dark little corridor started, panelled with boards. In the gradient of the wooden floor, there was a discernible even slope. Sidelnikov walked at least forty metres and the underground passage was still continuing. After another one hundred and fifty uncertain steps, he suddenly realised that he was already quite far from the hospital and tried to look at himself with the eyes of a stranger: a soiled bandage in place of the face, the prisoner's pyjamas and tattered institutional slippers. He looked liked an escaped convict ready for anything.

The underground passage came to an unexpected dead-end, a dirty streaked wall that Sidelnikov spotted from about ten metres away. To the left of the wall a dim doorway was visible. Despite the timid circumspection of his final twenty steps, he nearly stumbled upon the bare foot of a woman. Right in front of him, on the floor, a young woman was lying spread-eagled in a revealing position, stark naked with a gory gap in her underbelly. Sidelnikov jumped back, took a strained breath, and looked behind the doorjamb again. The dead body seemed languorous and warm, as if just out of bed. At the back of the larder-like room, there was another dead body, of a teenage girl that looked like a little skeleton covered with bluish goose-skin.

On his way back he was almost running, scared of meeting anyone alive. The visitors were still hanging about in the bay suspecting nothing. In the canteen, there was a rattle of dishes and the listless eating up of the watery porridge. The most astonishing thing was the *simultaneousness* of the events observed: *these* people were sitting here, while *those* were lying down there. The castle of the hospital was towering prim and proper over its putrid crypt, resting upon it like the only possible valid foundation.

The nights arrived at a snail's pace, struggling through the endless interval between supper, no more appetising than the intake of dispensed medicines, and the collective shutting down in compulsory hibernation, which started as if by command as soon as the white lights in wards and corridors were switched off centrally. However, the lamp with a yellow lampshade that was lit up on the desk of the duty nurse left a feeble hope that private life could still be lingering somewhere. The mornings were brought by force at six a.m. sharp, the lights and the radio – with the national anthem – were turned on everywhere possible. Sidelnikov, who had only managed to fall asleep a couple of hours before the anthem, was drawing his head in under the covers and making superhuman mental efforts to somehow approximate everything that "the great Russia united forever and ever" to his own fate, which appeared especially cumbersome and absurd in the mornings.

The women who shared the corridor with him brought the latest news items from everywhere and chewed them over to their hearts' content. The chief doctor's brother has left for Israel of his own accord; he's a traitor, now she might be sacked. Last night, a retired elderly lady was brought in, a hole in her head; her husband had an affair with his boss, the wife found out and phoned to complain and he hit her with something and was scared to call an ambulance, and now she is brought in, only she isn't breathing anymore, so there you are.

After some hesitation, for want of anything better to do, Sidelnikov decided to go down to the underground passage once again. The sense of danger stayed but was not as acute as before. The retired lady with the gash in her head, monumentally large, and with a garish manicure, was lying there, almost draped around a skinny hairy fellow tattooed from head to toe. The woman he saw before was not there. The goose-skin girl was still lying about, wanted by no one.

On the way back, he was straining to reconstruct the tragedy of the retired lady from the gleaned fragments: the future victim, stately as a monument to conjugal devotion, inserts a polished claw into the telephone dial while a heavy blunt object is biding its time, presumably somewhere in the kitchen. In the meantime, elsewhere, an unfamiliar hirsute criminal, with a fag between his teeth, is squandering the last day of his life before sprawling in profane post-mortem proximity to the noble corpse through the negligence of the hospital attendants.

...

There was almost no chance of any privacy in the hospital and therefore Sidelnikov became fond of daytime napping, into which he departed as if into an unoccupied territory, free from superfluous words and glances. He even developed a theory about why a human being actually needs sleep – at the very least, in order to be alone on a regular basis, to hear yourself out and to save yourself up. Without it, you could be simply pulled apart into pieces by mundane impressions and conversations.

'You've got a visitor. I think an actress!' For the very first time, curiosity shone through in the nurse's eyes.

Finding the "actress" in the crowded corridor was easy. Nadia was strolling to and fro as if on a catwalk, demonstrating her peerless legs, the short homemade manteau and outrageous make-up. She was immediately entranced by Sidelnikov's mask of a bandage.

'Wow! Mister X!' Nadia exclaimed attracting everybody's attention. '*My fate's to wear this mask forever!* Where could you smoke around here?'

Sidelnikov was not aware of a single place where it was allowed to smoke except the men's toilet, and so he decided to take his guest to the vault without showing her the mortuary. The mysterious darkness instantly inspired Nadia to strong actions such as a kiss on the neck, a show of lacy underwear and some free-style wrestling with the hospital pyjamas. By the by, Sidelnikov was informed that there was a new room found for him, and that both he and Shtrausenko were being summoned by the militia and that the Duchess of Alba had more to offer than just her armpits, please be fair, and that she admired him and missed him and that she was at present living in the flat of a friend who was away and the situation being as such, he was invited to come and see her, here's the address.

After Nadia's visit, the women he was sharing the corridor with started to cast meaningful glances at Sidelnikov. He was lying under the covers, apathetic in the midst of a bustling day, and repeating to himself like a child, 'I want to go home,' realising to his gradual consternation that there was nothing of the sort and the closest he had ever had to a "home" was Rosa's room in the communal flat in Shkiryatov Street.

It was already early November. It was time he got out of the hospital castle from where they were in no hurry to release him. During the rounds, the doctor would look from side to side absent-mindedly and repeat, 'It's a bit early yet,' without giving him even a rough date for discharge. Having found a good reason, Sidelnikov ambushed the doctor by his room:

'I can't afford to stay here for too long. I'm missing my classes.'

The doctor was silent for a little while and then laid down unexpected conditions:

'I'll discharge you, if you help us. As you know, we've got the celebrations coming up…'

'What celebrations?'

'How do you mean "What celebrations"? The Great October Revolution, of course. We need a wall newspaper done. Can you draw? There's paint and drawing paper in the doctor's room.'

The real challenge was inventing a title for the newspaper, which the doctor wanted to be both revolutionary and medical.

'Don't make it long,' he specified, 'it has to be brief, but celebratory.'

The creative process required no less than one and a half days, during which Sidelnikov pondered over about forty options. The pathos of revolutionary struggle clearly contradicted health care concerns, while medical practice had absolutely no need of victorious red banners.

At last, at daybreak of the fifth of November, just before the anthem, Sidelnikov was inspired. As soon as the lights were switched on centrally, he dashed to the doctor's room. The half-dried paint was the colour of cranberries. The dusty drawing paper did not want to unroll and strove to regain its cylindrical shape. However, already after breakfast, on a good one third of the sheet stretched out flat, his idea was splendidly displayed in bold and powerful words, "THE URGE". Unfortunately – or luckily – Sidelnikov's creation was either unnoticed or taken for granted, so that on the next day, the editor of "The Urge" was set free without further ado.

CHAPTER SIXTEEN

Trains bound for his hometown left daily, and this very fact provided a sort of lifeline for Sidelnikov. Whenever he had a chance, he would buy a ticket, reserved seat or third-class, put his clothes into a bag and go, even just for a few days. Since the reasons for leave inevitably turned out to be , if not university recesses, then public holidays (and even the most official ones, with parades and demonstrations, suited), every trip had an invariably festive feel to it.

Moreover, the trip was equivalent to evacuation from the hostel as the epicentre of an alcoholic explosion, where the critical mass of provincial gloom guaranteed the chain reaction of rage. Drinking parties swelled, outgrowing themselves, wrenched out the splintered rattling windows together with the frames, belched, rolled out into the corridors, slid down the railings and spread all over. Other people's beds in unlocked rooms were groaning under the burden of communal use. The faience sinks in lavatories and kitchens cracked like nuts. Hurling empty bottles along the whole length of the corridor was considered especially chic.

Leaving aside Sidelnikov's fondness for his trips and considering such trips from outside, it would be impossible to discover anything particularly joyful in them except perhaps the *anticipation* of joy. What could he be anticipating? Well, some extraordinary fellow travellers, for example. For the majority of passengers, the first, evening-time part of the journey comprised the hasty unrolling of terribly filthy mattresses on the rickety berths which were the colour of chocolate coated in dust, then making the bed with invariably wet and stained sheets acquired from the conductor after waiting in a half-alive queue, and the consumption of home-made food on a greasy newspaper powdered with breadcrumbs and salt.

'Going far?' he was asked by those who had a real chance to appear extraordinary, but did not take that chance and instead preferred to exchange strangers' news about the scarcity of food in shops, the prices of food, the quality of food, the harvest-time preserves for the winter, and food in general. Sidelnikov was prepared to endure this utter boredom, for the sake of a subsequent human conversation at the narrow little table underneath the dark window with the distant and near lights rushing towards the train. But more often than not, the interaction would be exhausted by the food theme, and people would hasten to turn in on their berths with faces as preoccupied as if it were time to fulfil some sacred duty.

Sidelnikov would go out for a smoke in the end of the corridor, dodging the potato-like bare heels that were sprouting on upper berths. For some reason, it was those cold smoky train corridors that he would remember best about his trips. Possibly, they represented his personal source of the iron patience which he needed so badly, and without which it was all too easy to give himself up to despair, or become addled by cowardly contempt towards people who were not guilty of anything, people who simply worked for the sake of food and therefore talked about it.

At a morning station, always the same one somewhere near the town of Kazhensk, a freckled deaf and dumb peddler of amateur photos would enter the carriage. The photos were offered furtively and therefore meant to be triply alluring. They were of subjects that were simply bound to appeal to any passenger – if not this one, then another: puppies and kittens of doll-like cuteness; similarly saccharine little girls with tiny bows enhanced by the wonders of photo-chemistry with cornflower-blue eyes and crimson lips against their grey-and-white little faces; a puffy infant with the Virgin; couples of cooing sweethearts; Stalin attired in his generalissimo uniform; the bronzed breasts of bikini-clad bathers.

The freckled peddler looked about when showing his prices on yellow fingers that had no nails. Once, he foisted a pack of cards on Sidelnikov and, with mad eyes, begged out of him his next-to-last two roubles. Afterwards, Sidelnikov could not decide for a long time what to do with that gang of thirty-six women clad in black stockings like a uniform, with smudged bewildered faces, ready for anything, thighs spread forever with identical diligence so that nobody would question their having a crotch.

His mother used to meet him with impetuous tenderness that however only lasted for the first day. Already on the next day, the relationship would become inflamed like sweaty skin rubbed sore. But to begin with, especially for the first two hours, everything would go exceptionally well. The loving mother would ladle out a bowl of borsch for her son, warning him to save space for the pelmeni to follow. Then she would sit down beside him and ask, 'So tell me!' Of course, the son had been ever such a good lad: he hadn't been sick once, he hadn't missed any classes, he had been eating properly at the canteen: first, second and third course; he didn't touch alcohol although he smoked; there were a lot of girls in his year but he hadn't yet made friends with any. Such information was balm for the soul and in its entirety would come handy for the official channels, that is, for his mother's telephone conversations with her friends. The speedy transformation of the good lad into scum of the earth and a scoundrel did not necessitate this information being modified a single bit.

Finally, it is time to mention that Lora was no longer living in the town. That was why such emptiness settled in the streets, stopping up his ears. After arranging to meet him by phone, the geographically constant Darya Konstantinovna handed Sidelnikov a letter in which Lora informed him of her decision to go away to live with her parents in Primorye at the seaside ("… they need my help and it will be easier for me, too") and asked him not to be sad or take her going away too tragically. He read and re-read the missive over and over again, not trusting his own eyes, trying to sniff out the faintest promise for the future between the lines – and he fancied he could sense it: 'I know you're good,' Lora had written, 'I rely on you.'

Strangely enough, the last phrase anticipated his current self-awareness. 'I rely on you' – he could have addressed himself like this too – 'on you alone because there is no one else.' He could no longer count on Rosa. When visiting Sidelnikov's dreams, she herself sometimes had a look of inscrutable hope, as if fulfilment of some unearthly needs of hers depended on him. What possible needs could the dead have?

Although unlikely that this was the precise moment of his definitive moving into adulthood, it was certainly the point of his ultimate loss of childhood as the time when it is okay to complain to anyone. Thus a sobbing child, utterly inconsolable just a moment ago, becomes quiet almost instantly once the grown-up listener to his sobs disappears out of his vision. Sidelnikov's solitary emotional experiences intensified at the very time he came to the clear realisation that the apparently profound feelings most people show to others were not meant for show at all.

But some things were absolutely not clear. For example, how he could cope with the shattering pity he felt for his mother, who was fading and losing her looks before his eyes and who strained her gaunt bosom with helpless and angry cries with or without a cause, and who was still completely hung up on her fights with her boss, the schoolmistress, and on what her girlfriends would say to her on the phone. Sidelnikov pitied his hometown, empty without his love, sad with the sadness of railway stations and poisoned with the fumes of industrial complexes where for the hazards of their labour, the workers were awarded bright honorary certificates and rust-coloured fringed pennants; his softly-spoken town cluttered at every corner with screaming statues in coats that were too tight and short. The last of such monuments, the most resplendent and hideous of all, would be erected in the centre of Komsomol Square opposite the Drama Theatre, when the Soviet regime was already declining. Its demise went almost unnoticed by the town's people, who were preoccupied with the extraordinary difficulties of redeeming rationing coupons for vodka, sugar, ciggies, sausages, cleaning materials and what have you.

Meanwhile, the town still measured up to its former self without losing any of its traits or indeed points of interest. The aroma of the famous offal pasties was as irresistible as before, the queue to the coveted steaming stall on the left bank across the bridge was as long and impatient as ever. The Old Town fried pasties successfully outlived both the construction of the happy future and all of the Kremlin old-timers, and even the change of the political system: a fact that made Sidelnikov muse abundantly on genuine historical values.

The town mythology was occasionally replenished by legends, mysterious but truthful to a degree. The "Bandeets" – pronounced with a heavy menacing stress on the second syllable – became one of those new legends. This was the name of a group of locals, who had suddenly grown fantastically, stunningly rich, as if they had discovered a whole river running with gold, but invisible to the outside world. According to the legend, the Bandeets had so much money that even the Caucasian market vendors, or the Director of the Industrial Complex for Trailers and Trolleys (that the enemy radio stations labelled "the world's largest tank building plant"), or even the First Secretary of the Communist Party Town Committee, looked destitute in comparison. However it came about, a limited contingent of closet Rockefellers was definitely present, and not just anywhere, but here, in this town, which could not but rouse plain curiosity at the very least.

During one summer holiday visit to his home town, on a hot day after the beach, Sidelnikov called at the "Around-the-Urals" tourist camp of which he had heard a lot as of a random fashionable leisure spot for "special people". In the centre of a balding lawn, bordered by wooden cabins with verandas, he met Sloth, the boss of the recording studio and the non-member of the trade union, lethargically sunning himself on a bath towel. Other holiday makers were out of sight, but from the cabin at the end of the row, the tipsy excited voices of several men and women could be heard. By the cabin porch, something incredible like a UFO was sitting right there in the dusty grass – a new Japanese tape-recorder. It was not merely that Sidelnikov had never dreamt of such a machine. It simply did not exist in his tangible world, probably just like the country of Japan itself. The massive sparkling contraption inscribed "Sharp" and carelessly left behind on the grass amazed and impressed by its very presence, but could hardly prove anything.

'Who's there in the cabin?' Sidelnikov asked Sloth.

'Why, it's them Bandeets over there,' answered Sloth so indifferently and casually as if he were talking of the tiny bluish black dragonflies flying around in exasperating quantities.

That first, invisible encounter with the Rockefellers ended abruptly half an hour later at the onset of sudden brutal rain that spared neither Sloth's towel, nor the UFO forgotten by its owners.

The second encounter during that same summer would end up with a complete overturning of Sidelnikov's already precarious lot.

CHAPTER SEVENTEEN

'Why don't you go to sleep?'

'I haven't yet learnt to sleep by your side.'

…

'Shall we have you come one more time, gently?'

'I'd rather stay where I am.'

'Well, shall I pretend that I'm asleep, and you will…'

'As a special agent!'

'Or a maniac rapist… I would really like to hold back as long as possible, 'cause as soon as you came today, I did too, I rushed…'

Did he and Lora really have conversations like that? Did they really talk this happy nonsense? Did they just. And the feverish whispering, with the apple breath flowing from mouth to mouth, and the pungent odour of their mutual love sweat were more real than this eyeless mummified separation. But even when Sidelnikov unexpectedly fathomed the horrible thing that would have been better not known by anyone, he still did not stop aching for Lora. And what he fathomed was that, at the end of the day, no-one really chooses anyone in particular, so in place of the one and only sweetheart, there could have been somebody else – and here's the horror – just about *anybody* else.

...

He was now sharing a room with chemistry students. They treated Sidelnikov and all others in the humanities rather like some profoundly military people treat civilians: *civvies* – what could one expect from them? However, there wasn't any strong front-line camaraderie amongst the chemistry students either, everyone kept themselves to themselves, there were no feasts or even a common kettle. In the evenings, Sidelnikov would have tea on the fifth floor with the Turkmens who all of a sudden took a liking to him. The Turkmens were such a tight-knit bunch that it was impossible to meet them separately. When they were running down the stairs from their top-floor rooms with the gradual crescendo of stomping it was like a herd of lathery horses and it was safer to step aside. In the course of tea-drinking, the herd leader, Allayarov, elicited from Sidelnikov the particulars of his skirmish with Shtrausenko and said quietly upon emptying his third cup of tea:

'I'll morder him.'

The most unpleasant memory was the trip Sidelnikov and Shtrausenko made to the militia as per the summons. Sidelnikov was walking on one side of the street whereas the watchman, tail between his legs, was walking on the opposite side. The charming lady investigator met them with the vile question:

'Well, have you settled everything between yourselves?'

'I have got nothing to settle with him!' Sidelnikov was so indignant that he became bombastic like a communist.

'Well then, are you going to file a complaint?'

'No…'

'Why "no"?' cried the lady investigator.

'I feel sorry for him.'

When they were coming out of the room, Shtrausenko looked both triumphant and insolent. With hindsight, Sidelnikov could not sensibly explain to himself the cause of the wretched spur-of-the-moment "feeling sorry". And in reply to Allayrov's "I'll morder him" he just gave a wave of the hand, meaning: the last thing anyone wants is to go to prison because of that turd.

A month later, when the watchman nipped into a bathroom for a drink of water and bent over the tap, which he turned upside down to make a drinking fountain, an unidentified malefactor came up to him from behind and bashed him on the back of his head with such force that Shtrausenko's teeth were crushed against the cold metal. The watchman was weeping and spitting blood and saying that somebody had taken revenge on him for his vigilant service at the hostel lobby. The avenger was never found but Sidelnikov strongly suspected a trace of Turkmen.

Something was happening with Nadia. She left the hostel and was now calling in as if on an excursion to a reservation of poor, but proud, Red Indians. Her moods soared, or blazed, or plummeted. At times, she would even grow indifferent to her appearance and clothes. She would fade, her face darkened as if she was burnt out inside. In his mind, Sidelnikov called this "internal combustion" and secretly feasted his eyes on Nadia, but would forget her as soon as she was gone. Once, for instance, he found two small cold tangerines under his pillow, but could not guess who they were from.

Nadia often asked Sidelnikov "to walk her" and he dutifully, if not very willingly, complied with her requests. He picked all the best places for walking her: the railway station, or a greasy spoon in Pushkin Street that was crammed and grubby but famous for its hand-made pelmeni. Once, Nadia dragged him into the flat of a girlfriend who was away at the time. There he enjoyed a bubble bath (a rare treat for a hostel resident), had two helpings of Russian salad and, with the words, "much, much obliged", scarpered despite the invitation to stay overnight – or forever. This dwelling put him off by its indistinct resemblance to the home of Darya Konstantinovna. But back there Lora and he were standing embracing each other in the middle of the room, anxious not to touch even the mere surface of somebody else's life, whereas here, a semi-naked Nadia was lying on the orphaned sofa with a cigarette, with her wondrous ballet-or-circus legs up in the air. The legs were admirable, but this did not mean that he wanted to come and live in a circus.

...

'Well, Nadia, where would you like to live?'

The people queuing for pelmeni were staring at Nadia like some exotic creature, with almost animal curiosity and, for some reason, with fear. Sidelnikov had a thought that the most dazzling beauty is scary, being obviously unapproachable, and therefore as often as not doomed to be unclaimed and, ultimately, unwanted by anyone.

'I'd like to live in Venice. Or in Genoa.'

Shiny stains from spilled vinegar were drying on the table.

'Because ours is shit and not a normal country. Why don't you say anything? C'mon, say at least that you disagree!'

'I disagree.'

The pelmeni were gone before the hunger.

'I'd like to have your baby.'

'It is the government that's shit, not the country.'

'I wouldn't even bother you about paternity. This child would be mine only.'

'Well, what about me? A stud, and it's over?'

'You'll never have any money. Would you buy me more juice please? Don't be upset. You know no-one can earn anything here, unless you do black market.'

'There's no apple juice left, only pomegranate and it's really sour.'

'You know, I'm going to have to get married, for the housing registration.'

Soon afterwards, it turned out that there already existed a contender who was giving her no peace and was practically treading on her heels, ready for anything. When Nadia called Sidelnikov long-distance since he was as usual spending the holidays in his hometown, he could not help asking out of curiosity:

'How is your housing registration doing?'

'There he is, outside the post office for the past half-hour.'

Igor Sakhnovsky

...

The summer was going wild in the town as if before an eternal winter or on the eve of doomsday. The shabbiest little parks and gardens let themselves go, breaking into rampant blooming, surrendering their leaves and countless petals to obliteration by the heat, brief powerful showers and renewed waves of heat. Come evening, Sidelnikov was longing to get out he knew not where, but at least out of the house and out of himself. In the twilight, he walked through the Park "of Culture and Leisure" overgrown with black currants and honeysuckle, through the lingering fragrance of maize pollen, to the slowly cooling asphalt of Komsomol Square, every time imagining himself a participant in indescribable adventures that were always too late and could never get started.

The weary town went to bed early. The more provoking seemed the late-night rumble of a band emanating from the "Jasper" café. A red-faced bouncer in an Army coat minus the epaulets was looking around just waiting to pour scorn on those longing to enter. In the street, a few of the excluded from the merry-making were hanging about pleadingly. Sidelnikov quickened his pace and assuming a purposeful air circumvented the red mug before the latter had time to react. Yet once inside where it was hot and noisy, Sidelnikov realised that the effort was pointless. About forty people, utterly rampageous, like first-year pupils without their teacher's supervision, were jumping and stomping near the half-ravaged tables in time to the brutally loud thump from wardrobe-like speakers which fenced the semi-circular stage with the band members:

The Vital Needs Of The Dead

I cannot speak for the whole of Odessa,
The whole of Odessa is so very big!

Sidelnikov felt slightly lost, not knowing where
to perch himself, but almost immediately, a sweaty
wench in a tight lacy dress leapt out of the dancing
throng, grabbed his hand and pulled him into the
middle. He made a clumsy attempt at adapting
to everyone else's bodily movements but, at that
moment, the song about Odessa ended and the
public surged back towards the unfinished drinks.
The lacy wench with a hot wine-smelling exhalation
of "Come and join us!" steered Sidelnikov to the
table where her crowd was sitting. Instantly, he
had a full glass and a huge plate with meat was
pushed towards him. It was a birthday party for
the glamorous tall blonde sitting at the head of
the table. While a young man with a golden fang
shining in his mouth, resembling the famous rogue
Ostap Bender, was proposing a toast, Sidelnikov
looked about. Bottles of unfamiliar imported
vodka and dry martini, five or six types of sausage,
caviar, some black meat – nothing of the kind could
be found on any other table in the café, let alone
anywhere within thousands of miles of the reality
surrounding them. A fat fellow with a childish
haircut refilled Sidelnikov's glass and candidly
complained, 'Lyusia's been pestering me 'cause
she'd like another fur coat… I goes, Haven't we got
enough fur coats already, let's get you those rings
with nice little stones instead?' Then he added in
confidential whisper, 'But you know what, this fur
coat is re-e-ally something!' Lyusia, who sported a
delicate boyish moustache, hurried the gathering
and reminded that they were in for a "tsar bathing".

The birthday girl, called Valentina, was glowing pink and divinely scented – she hailed from those bosomy Flemish paintings and the kingdom of haberdashery.

'Are you coming with us for the "tsar bathing"?' asked the lacy wench.

Sidelnikov nodded. He was led along by apathetic curiosity and did not feel like changing course.

In the lobby by the public phone, the red-faced bouncer, unprompted, obsequiously offered Sidelnikov a two-kopecks coin for the telephone, and Sidelnikov rang his mother to say that he would be out with some friends till late, maybe until morning. His mother snorted and slammed the phone down.

The gold-toothed Bender stopped two taxis in one go. They loaded in, cheerful and self-important. Lyusia and the lacy one were squabbling about who was going to sit next to Sidelnikov. The cars ripped through the sleeping town like fire engines to a fire.

CHAPTER EIGHTEEN

In the dark, the river was taut and warm. It smelled of freshly washed linen, the silent work of a hundred thousand invisible laundresses.

Upon the command, "Girls to the left, boys to the right", Sidelnikov deduced that the "tsar bathing" required stripping to the skin. The taxi drivers waiting behind the bushes were talking in an undertone. 'That's them Bandeets, innit?' one of them uttered a familiar phrase.

The intimate touch of water brought goosebumps rushing on his skin. Entering the flowing darkness up to his chest, Sidelnikov pushed the bottom with his feet and dived. If it were not for the tightness in his lungs, he could have, without coming to the surface, torn along the river merging with his body and then finally flowed into the open sea, as into a non-scary and logical death. He sensed that he had swum out too far and resurfaced reluctantly. The surface was cooler than the depths. Before diving again, he aimed at the voices of the bathers, turning his back to the unattainable sea.

And once more, Sidelnikov was swimming for a long time, oblivious to everything until an underwater collision with an unfamiliar smooth nakedness made him jump to the surface, touching the shallow bottom with his toes. In the process, Sidelnikov's stomach crushed heavily against a tall woman standing with her back to him. She uttered a startled sound and laughed in Valentina's voice, but instantly stopped laughing and went quiet without making any attempt to move away. Thereupon Sidelnikov was powerfully dragged in by drunken desire, just for five blind seconds which, however, were long enough for pressing against the yielding and supple back and the generously proffered behind and for repeating the wild belly thrust barely hindered by the thin layer of water between flesh and flesh.

Somehow coping with trouser-legs and the sticky sand on his feet, he despised himself for the thief-like haste, but for some reason he felt that he must get dressed before the others reached the shore. On the contrary, when the others came out, they were in no hurry, joking and having a smoke as if it was not night time and there were no cab meters ticking away behind the bushes.

Dressed, Valentina transformed back into the birthday girl and the opulent haberdashery queen whom Sidelnikov would not dare approach. She came up to him herself, deliberately clumsy in her high heels over the sand, her eyes shining, full of the dark river, and leaned powerfully on his forearm.

'Tomorrow morning, stay in bed – do not get up till everyone's gone. OK?'

And immediately after that, without any transition, the conspiratorial whisper rose to an exclamation:

'Lena, have you seen my necklace?'

'I haven't seen nothing!' the lacy wench, still unbuttoned, replied with hostile emphasis.

The part of town they rushed to after the beach – a cluster of tower blocks amidst a boundless wasteland – was not familiar to Sidelnikov. Valentina lived in a three-room apartment, apparently on her own. In the sitting room, there was no furniture at all apart from an enormous electric fireplace and a heavy rug on the floor from wall to wall, on which the guests reclined like patricians, to round off the orgy. The choice of delicacies was reduced to smoked sausage and vodka. They were reclining for about half an hour, exchanging infrequent lazy words, almost without looking at each other, as happens in a tightly knit circle. 'Like in a gang,' thought Sidelnikov.

The rest of the night he spent tossing and turning in the thick of the laborious snoring and wheezing of the male half of the gang. The ladies were sleeping in the next room. It was already getting light behind the net curtains when he rebuked himself, yet again, for leading an obviously erroneous lifestyle – and then fell asleep with a clear conscience.

According to his impression, everybody was astir in about a second later, and the fat bloke asked his spouse Lyusia for some champagne in the bright voice of a boy scout. In his mind, Sidelnikov set the alarm to "complete silence" and, ever so diligent, got back to sleep. It was silence that woke him up. There was not a soul in sight. He pricked up his ears: there was the noise of water running in the bathroom.

Half a year later, having played back that day like a film, he would try to identify the ratio of accidental and inevitable in it. Could Valentina, who was practically a stranger to him, NOT offer him, a stranger, what she did offer him, risking her head? Or were the several hours in a hot whipped up bed capable of being so crucial? Could he have consented right away rather than brush it aside, engulfed, or well-nigh swallowed up by her naked and substantial charms?

What Valentina said when she next had a chance to catch her breath after – what was it, the fourth ascent? – could be summed up as follows: was it truly Sidelnikov's place to live among the poor and forever watch every penny? She'd rather work with him than with those dolts. The work was just taking some stuff to and from Moscow and

Leningrad. And to keep mum, of course. And he could finish his studies afterwards. But at least he would have anything he could wish for.

'C'mon, tell me, what would you like? How about a house by the sea?'

But on the screen of his memory, Sidelnikov was plainly bored when the talk was about money and seaside homes. What he was really fascinated by at that moment was the inscrutability of the naked body lying next to him, its beautifully groomed taut whiteness and fragrant folds. He was stunned by the contrast between the pampered smoothness of the groin and the just visible scarlet of the shameless wild meat. And when this handsome large woman abandoning herself to him was crying out in an unexpectedly high-pitched and piercing voice, he had to unwillingly assume the role of a torturer whose absolute cool-headedness would probably be pitied by a seasoned executioner.

Leaving, he promised to call her but she said, 'I've got no phone in this flat, you can come round just like that,' and wrote down her address on a page from a notebook. Then from her bedroom she brought a tiny parcel which looked like a tightly packed deck of cards and put it in the pocket of his summer jacket: 'Here's a little souvenir for you.' When Sidelnikov was already going down the stairs, she called him back and handed him some small blue coupons, 'Pay the cab driver with these instead of money.' For some reason, it was then that he thought he was never to see her again.

The day, windy and hot, was languishing, swaying from side to side, uncertain of where to lean apart from the inexorable twilight. Sidelnikov crossed the wasteland and was walking along the road at random. Soon, a dust-covered taxi flew towards him as if on call.

The driver was chain-smoking and turning the controls of his radio. Through the noise, the song "Hope" was seeping through.

> *One just has to learn how to wait,*
> *One will have to be calm and tenacious...*

Sidelnikov attempted to adopt a calm and tenacious expression and closed his eyes. The sharply blowing draught in the back seat was ruthlessly tousling his hair, threatening to scatter his brains, but it was pleasant to have the wind on his face. The last verse of the song sounded puzzling because of its rather grim graveyard imagery:

> *The unknown star up in the sky*
> *Is shining like a monument to Hope.*

"If hope did not die then pray, why is there a monument to it?" Searching for cigarettes, Sidelnikov found Valentina's present in his pocket. The bundle was securely cellotaped over so he had to tear the cover. For a few moments, he was gazing like an idiot at the bas-relief profile of Lenin, whereupon he quickly put everything back into his pocket. The "present" turned out to be a bundle of ten-rouble notes, the entire bank-wrapped pack of one grand.

His first impulse was to shout to the driver to go back: with a face of stone, Sidelnikov would ring the doorbell to Valentina's flat and return the money.

She would try to say something but he would leave in silence. Then it occurred to him that such a present appeared absurd and even insulting – unless Valentina was inviting Sidelnikov to join her in her mysterious enterprise. So it looked like she was securing his consent. In any case, he could come and visit her in a couple of days in order to return the bills and clear up the situation.

He strained his imagination, trying to animate the gigantic mass of money with three naughts deposited in his pocket but could not remember a single temptation in any shop that would have a matching price tag. Mopeds, motorbikes and other vehicles did not stir Sidelnikov. Then suddenly he recalled an account of a Mediterranean cruise he heard from a fellow train passenger. True that the narrator mostly concentrated on the foreign prices and the circumstances of purchasing some marvellous mohair, but Sidelnikov was sufficiently impressed by the geographical list heard from a live witness: Marseilles, Barcelona, Naples, Crete, Malta, Alexandria... It was not just that the names attracted him by their exotic novelty – on the contrary, to him they were very well-known and even familiar. For instance, he would repeat a hundred times the poem about "a blue island – the green Crete", imagining in dazzling details the encounter of the two great lovers that took place in Alexandria nineteen centuries ago, but there you are, the chatter of an ordinary woman in a second-class carriage, who broke a heel of her sandal on the warm dented flagstones of the Palace of Knossos was as convincing and amazing as the testimony of ancient authors, perhaps even more so.

One of the passengers asked a down-to-earth question about the cost of the cruise. The woman said that the price of the package was eight hundred roubles and the wonder immediately acquired the enormous factual equivalent, namely, twenty times Sidelnikov's monthly grant (or his mother's salary for more than half a year), and on top, he'd have no money for food and accommodation!

When Komsomol Square came in sight, Sidelnikov asked the driver to pull in and gave him the little blue coupons that had got all sweaty in his palm. The driver nodded with discernible respect.

Before returning home, he felt he had to relieve somehow this unmotivated surge of energy – to cross the square with a light step, to circumvent, almost at a run, the lifeless bulk of the Drama Theatre, to go deep into the park without hiding his idiotic grin. "A blue island – the green Crete" was the most accurate name of and keyword to this bliss. The park was still immersed in its grass-and-berry evaporations, not a bit different from the previous evening, as if a night and a day had not passed, but the same evening was still continuing. It was Sidelnikov who had befallen a change, and he was struggling to grasp its elusive nature. 'One would think it was because of this somebody else's money...' – the thought was clumsy and a bit shameful. He shoved his hand into his pocket once again and froze.

The money was not in his jacket. Not in any of the pockets. Nor in his trouser pockets, except for his own six roubles and twenty kopecks. Dashing back, towards the square, was necessary to set his mind at ease, more than for anything else. The cab would have already gone, with the money on its back seat. Possibly, another passenger would find it. There was an icy logic in what had happened and the only thing it dictated to Sidelnikov was that on the following day he would have to go and see Valentina.

His mother met him in silence and did not offer him any supper.

He drank some cold tea and got undressed, then was re-reading Wilhelm Hauff's fairy-tales till half past midnight.

A stranger in a red cloak, his face was completely hidden, was waiting for the wretch by the parapet of the Ponte Vecchio. Slowly, he said, 'Follow me!' The campaniles of Florence struck the irreversible hour, and the spring of the tale, about a chopped-off hand that did not offer any clues or outcomes, uncoiled with a hiss.

Rosa appeared most hurriedly as if, preoccupied with an urgent matter, she had been waiting for Sidelnikov to finally get to sleep. At last, as he appeared in the domain of sleep where she could reach him, she told him with greatest clarity and firmness, 'Don't even think about it! Neither tomorrow, nor at any other time...' He had never seen Rosa so worried and hastened to calm her down. He said, here in Florence we have no other options, everything has already happened, that is, it's already too late, I am the one to know, the circumstances are absolutely fatal... But she interrupted him almost rudely, 'Look here, stop beating about the bush. This is not what I'm talking about!' It was implied without further explanations that she was talking about the woman called Valentina, and nobody else. Even though Sidelnikov slept till quite late, almost until noon, the only substantial remnant of his dream was Rosa's warning shout that gained the strength of an order, 'DON'T EVEN THINK ABOUT IT!'

When he was washing his face, he spotted his shirt, newly laundered and hung on the line in the bathroom. He felt with his fingers in the wet breast pocket – and found nothing.

In the kitchen, his mother was sealing jars of raspberry preserve. Before asking her the hopeless question, Sidelnikov stood by the window for a little while, dipped his glance into the enamelled basin filled with raspberry mash and watched a little fly resting on its syrupy edge.

'Have you seen a piece of paper with an address?'

'Whose address?'

It seemed to him that the question did not surprise her.

'Well, there was that little piece of paper. In my shirt pocket…'

'Well, whose address was it?'

He no longer wanted to ask her. He did not feel like sharing the fate of the little fly that came to a sticky end.

After two empty days, he left for Srednovsk.

Igor Sakhnovsky

CHAPTER NINETEEN

If not for Professor Dergunov, Sidelnikov would have never chanced upon those wonderful golden-and-purple pieces of glass that let any human see with their own eyes utterly indescribable, inordinately beautiful and fearsome things.

It is hard to tell exactly what it was that the old professor had against his student. It might be that the fatal reason for Dergunov's antipathy was the insufficient rapture and the lack of reverence on Sidelnikov's face during those sacred moments when the University patriarch was affectionately narrating to the green first-year students his cherished reminiscences of his years of friendship with the great Urals storyteller Pazhov. At that time, Pazhov had not yet grown a long folklore beard, he was wearing a leather jacket and carrying a gun and was granted the right to shoot on the spot at any socially dubious characters. Although the fighting past of the professor himself was not as romantic and fancy-dress, however, the distinguished snitch Dergunov helped to put away a few of his fellow university teachers in earnest and for the long haul, which was known to almost everyone in the department. Therefore, Sidelnikov, as a listener, was committing precarious nonchalance by not feigning admiration and by making no facial efforts at all.

'Tell me who was the theorist and the leader of the "natural school"?' asked Dergunov.

He was staring intently at the delicate baby-pink fingernails of his left hand whilst keeping his right hand under the table. The exam was almost over. Sidelnikov, who gave extensive answers to both questions of the examination paper, felt that he definitely earned a "four" out of five.

'Belinsky.'

Dergunov nodded.

'Belinsky was the theorist. And who was the leader?'

Sidelnikov hesitated. It was news to him that Belinsky could cede to anybody else his role as the leader of such a dull undertaking as the "natural school". Gogol's magnificent figure was shimmering in the not so distant background, even if he was at that time in Italy, and Sidelnikov was a bit reluctant to involve Gogol in this palaver anyway. But the delicate senile fingernails bode foul play.

'Gogol?''

'Oh! Then you are not familiar with Gogol's life, are you?' Dergunov exclaimed, visibly pleased. 'At that time, Nikolai Vassilyevich was living abroad. You may go. Un-sa-tis-fac-tory. And do not even hope for a good mark, until… Russian literature is not what you imagine.'

Upon coming out of Dergunov's room, Sidelnikov leafed through the textbook in utter boredom and disgust. "Vissarion Belinsky, bla, bla, bla… refuted accusations of reactionary critics in defence of …bla, bla, bla…the "natural school", whose leader and theorist he was". So he was indeed both the leader and the theorist! In translation into the Prosecutor's language of Fate, it meant that Sidelnikov was doomed to fail this test and, through this, the whole of winter exams and, ultimately, to end up on the aforementioned railway station bench for those permanently in transit or homeless. He was doomed for sure because the Professor failed him, the half-wit, on purpose, by just a single weightlessly elegant gesture. And indeed, why on earth should the distinguished brother-in-arms of the KGB storyteller be untrue to his signature elegance?

There was one week left until the end of the exams. Twice, squirming inside with humiliation, Sidelnikov came up to Dergunov in the corridor with the request to re-sit the exam and both times he was met with righteous indignation: 'There are such gaps in your knowledge! And you are in such a rush! Well, I doubt if you can pass it at all…'

Everything was going precisely according to the evil plan, but then a flu epidemic meddled with Fate. The philology patriarch got mighty snivels and took sick leave. Pochinyaev, a youthful senior lecturer of the same subject, effortlessly passed Sidelnikov with a "good" mark, marvelling at his failed first attempt. The bench in the railway station remained vacant. However, his grant for the next six months gave up the ghost.

…

By that time, Sidelnikov had successfully mastered a sport, novel to him – namely, surviving on one rouble a day. To be achieved, this required heroic self-restraint and most accurate calculations because, for example, one day's lapse represented by a set of postcards with reproductions of impressionist paintings cancelled all rights to the next day's lunch. And such profligacy as tinned fish in tomato sauce or even, God forbid, in oil, threw several kilos of potatoes out of his budget.

The loss of his grant spurred on the challenge to find employment. The career of a night watchman was not to happen, thwarted by the prevalence of faster and luckier place-seekers. Sidelnikov nearly began thinking of getting a job loading freight trains when the poet Yuri, who was in his year, offered him the position of evening sweeper at a secret optics factory which the poet had recently infiltrated in the same sweeping capacity.

Sweeping the rubbish together in the deserted workshops in the evening was conducive to heart-to-heart conversations on global culture. The partners in conversation would talk to each other approximately like this: 'You see, old man…', 'Yes, old man, you are absolutely right…' Something had to be urgently done with global culture.

Being a family man, Yuri would usually hurry up with the job in order to leave early. Sidelnikov would be left on his own on the whole of the secret territory and undertake unauthorised excursions. This was how he chanced upon the rubbish bins. This rubbish deposit was different from an ordinary stinking garbage can because it was clean or, you could even say, pristine. It was because it contained hundreds of various sized glass pieces and lenses, rejected due to minuscule chips or scratches. The only time Sidelnikov had experienced a similar ecstasy was when Rosa and he used to visit the haberdashery shop "to have a glance at the diamonds". Splashes and drops frozen in flight, polished to a mirror shine as if delicately licked by a divinity and now shimmering violet gold on the bottom of a rubbish bin – they only needed someone to rest his naked eye fearlessly against their smoothness and be stunned, dazzled by the sight of a totally different life, that is an altogether separate universe, located not elsewhere but just here.

Mind-blown, Sidelnikov seriously contemplated plundering a few bits of the precious garbage with the aim to further the rapture, but he was thwarted by the honest and defenceless eyes of the armed security guard by the name of Sofia Karpovna whom he had to pass at the exit, as well as by the memory of a strict paper signed hastily that obliged the "auxiliary worker" G. F. Sidelnikov to keep the defence-and-optics secrets safe.

Soon the sweepers' night shift was changed to daytime and pensioners replaced the students. Sidelnikov had to part with the glass treasures but by no means with rubbish tips. He became an orderly at the trauma unit of the First City Hospital where they already knew him and accepted him as one of their own. They even allocated to him a personal office (in the bathroom) and entrusted him with a numbered mop, a bucket and plastic bags for all sorts of rubbish.

The word "orderly" was only pretending to have any order in it. Anything within the official duties of the newly appointed medical worker reeked of stale blood, ammonia and iodine, spittle and cigarette butts floating in urine. From an orderly's point of view, the patients were doing nothing but fouling. Some endeavoured to make use of Sidelnikov's "office" at the most unsuitable times. For some reason, women almost never bothered to hide their pale nakedness and sometimes, Sidelnikov imagined himself a voyeur in the deliberate disguise of an orderly.

Outside in the cold, running out of the hospital building with the fifth or sixth huge bag of rubbish, he caught himself feeling insensitive and numb, as if under narcosis. After work, in the crowded tram on the way to his hostel pillow, this narcosis continued to work, obscuring, like a heaving wave, the nest of the forbidden hatchling who was destined to suffer. In this state of mind, at the crossing of The 8th of March Street and Decembrists' Street, Sidelnikov nearly got run over by a car with Nadia in the front passenger seat wearing a man's black hat with a lowered brim under whose shadow only her lips could be seen, outlined in bold lipstick. Or maybe it was not Nadia, but someone who looked just like her... In the grocery shop, he bought a jar of tomato sauce, to put on bread for breakfast and supper, and walked two blocks, struggling to recall Nadia's phrase that got stuck in his mind like a splinter. The wind was blowing into his back as if pushing him to do something self-evident. The faces of passers-by walking against the wind all had an identical expression of suffering distress. Finally, he remembered. Nadia had said, "You will never have any money". He wondered if this was written all over him.

When Sidelnikov was unable to sort things out within his own soul, he applied a self-made remedy that he deemed infallible. One only had to listen carefully to one's very first morning thought when only just awake, with the eyes still closed. At such a moment, his secluded soul would blab, being only half-awake, and it was possible to seize the end of the tangled thread. To his surprise, in a few winter mornings, Sidelnikov caught Valentina in his thoughts. He was thinking of her as a woman, with keen desire but without any perceptible symptoms of the love anguish he was inured to by Lora. In one of his morning visions (on the theme of Turkish janissaries for some reason), the inflamed sabre steel was piercing – however, bloodlessly – a submissive European slave woman, moaning in the high-pitched voice of Valentina's… All of a sudden, effortlessly, her surname surfaced in his memory – Likhter – even though he had only heard it once when Valentina mentioned her ex-husband: her "old pot and pan" had suddenly gone to pot, leaving behind nothing but his surname.

Now Sidelnikov could find her address. All he needed to start the mechanism for the change of his lot (not necessarily for the better, but *some change* for sure) would be a mere sixteen hours on the train and a short wait at the inquiry office.

Yet he did not let himself to hurry. He waited out four cold weeks, endured an hour-long queue to the railway ticket office, thriftily spaced out three cabbage pies and a Garcia Marques novel over the whole journey, gratified his mother with a summary of his inexhaustible accomplishments in studies, stayed at home for two days without budging out and at last, halfway between the bakery and the greengrocer's, honoured the inquiry office with his visit.

He was staggered by the thick crowd of visitors, clearly his fellow hopefuls in the change of fate. The girl at the counter had ink-stained fingers and the sad little face of a diligent underachiever. Upon passing to her the form with the full name of his quarry, Sidelnikov did not make a pest of himself, peeping under her hand as everybody else did while she was leafing through her thick registry volumes – instead he turned away with a look of boredom. He could not risk revealing his pursuit to Fate.

The girl was leafing through the books, then was telephoning somewhere but he had his eyes glued to the wall painted lifeless green, until suddenly he felt a gentle tap of the ink-stained little fingers on his hand – the way someone would touch when they do not wish to startle you or draw the attention of the people around.

On the scrap of paper that was handed over to Sidelnikov in considerate silence, a crooked single word was scribbled, non-existent in any language but brought forth by the solecistic labour of the underachiever, the diabolic omniscience of the office and, perhaps, the immutability of Fate:

IMPRIZEND.

CHAPTER TWENTY

In the centre of a small public garden between the Opera House and the University where Sidelnikov was studying there stood on a pedestal the cast iron Bolshevik Srednov, whose name was patiently borne by the huge city like an undersized second-hand jacket. The rebellious Srednov was cast in the unhinged pose of a street punk, which did not go together with his round spectacles and goatee. On the left, the square was watched over by the clumsy pasty-white muses on the pediment of the Opera House and on the right, by senile portraits of the Politburo members hung on the University façade in honour of public holidays and left there for a long time until the cleanly shaven and well-groomed images turned grim with bad weather. It was clear that they would never die and even if such a misfortune did strike, a new cohort would have had enough time to grow as decrepit.

Needless to say, in this sickly company supervising Sidelnikov's solitary walks, Rosa's shadow would have been least appropriate, being as she was a lively and unconstrained substance. Yet it was here that after ten o'clock one December evening, Sidelnikov heard with his own ears a phrase spoken behind his shoulder by the cool dear voice he could not have confused with anybody else's in the world.

Soft snow was falling, lit up by the yellow glow of streetlights. Annoyed with himself, Sidelnikov turned his head and naturally saw nobody nearby. By the way, if that was indeed a hallucination, it was not just an aural one, since the words were accompanied by a soft steaming exhalation from the mouth of the speaker.

The day had already run out. It was time to go back to the hostel. But what Rosa told him implied that he should go to Nizhny Gravesk that very evening. Strictly speaking, it was only the name of the place that was completely audible, whereas the whole phrase sounded like a vague, but urgent, plea. Something like, 'Please go, you still have the time!' or 'let's go together...' In short, utter absurdity. Besides, not knowing a soul in the Northern gulag-and-industrial town of Nizhny

Gravesk, Sidelnikov had never been there, nor ever aspired to go, and altogether could not imagine anything in the nearest future apart from the winter night. 'Yeah, just like that, get up and go, as if I've nothing else to do!' he was squabbling under his breath with God knows who, heading down the main street to the trolley bus stop, more and more looking like the village idiot in his own eyes. A half-empty trolley bus bound for the station pulled up and opened its doors for Sidelnikov. Such courtesy was hard to resist.

He melted the thin mica-like sparkly ice crust on the glass with his fingers – seen through these tiny dactyloscopic portholes, buildings and streets appeared somehow different, cosier and closer.

The railway station was all astir. Besides the clichéd partings and meetings, there was a constant and inexorable atmosphere of uncertainty, be that happy or hopeless. It was probably tiredness that made Sidelnikov feel like he was drifting as if he had drunk a glass of Agdam, the "fruit-and-berry wine", on an empty stomach. In this state – also known as "automatic pilot" – he managed, even without a ticket, to get a decent seat, and by the window into the bargain, in the third-class carriage of a northbound train. His sobering up was facilitated by the loud-mouthed conductor who made him pay her a fine – or possibly a bribe – notifying him in return that the journey to Gravesk was less than three hours long.

This length of time was more than enough for him to do a mental conversion of the sum paid to the conductor into meat pies and cigarettes, get terribly frozen and curse everything on earth. 'What the hell? Where on Earth am I going?' Therefore, upon arrival at his idiotic destination, the now completely sober Sidelnikov first dashed to the ticket office of Nizhny Gravesk station, to inquire about the time of the next train to Srednovsk and buy a ticket. It turned out that he could go back in fifty minutes. This reassuring prospect generated a desire, quite normal in a leisurely tourist, to go and have a look at the unknown town.

He came out in the cold from the back of the station and looked around. A blind snowy wasteland separated the station from distant dwellings that had very few lights. The populated part of the landscape looked a tiny trifle surrounded by the land which stretched out under the snow and the irresponsive black sky. The night had withdrawn too deeply into itself – no point calling it back or shaking it awake. Despite the immensity of the space, only the merciless cold made itself comfortable there, grandly and without restraint.

Thus having looked round the town and become so frozen as to completely lose any touristic inclinations, Sidelnikov returned to the station, intending not to stick his nose out again before the train arrived. The waiting room was impressive by its institutional starkness and the majestic remnants of the Stalin empire style: a ceramic tile floor as in public lavatories, a ceiling with grimy grey stucco mouldings of wheat ears and sickles. From the oval niche in the wall, Lenin painted in imitation ivory was walking out half a step. A pair of columns in the same colour supported a high gallery with round-bellied balusters that could have served as a rostrum for the Leader, had he finally decided to leave his niche. But right at that moment, a one-legged old cripple was standing at the banisters, sending drunken curses into the void. In one corner of the room, someone was asleep on a spread-out newspaper, resting his head on some packs. Another three and half people including Sidelnikov hung around by the walls, shivering from the chill.

The cripple on the gallery was making more of a spectacle of himself. Having cast aside his crutch, he grasped the banister with both hands and continued screaming obscenities. This one-man show went on for the benefit of an almost entirely empty auditorium, where the few odd spectators turned away pretending not to hear. But it looked like the old man did not need an audience. With white-hot hoarseness and life-threatening strain, he was presenting to his country, and indeed the whole world, his lifelong hurt that could not be appeased. The proclaimed list of wrongdoers included: sons of bitches, bloody bastards, prison snitches, pigs, fucking communists and General Secretary Brezhnev. One could almost say it was the last scream on the gallows.

Rather pusillanimously, Sidelnikov had a fleeting thought about the old man being easy prey for the vigilant authorities, very likely exhausted by their energetic idleness. But what good was to them this cripple: he was not the type for a secret report. While on the contrary, any chatty student...

What happened within the next three seconds was as rapid as an avalanche. Resting his weight on his left leg, the old man swung his right thigh with the peg leg over the banister, slid along it on his stomach – and threw himself down with a jerk. But even as the suicide was rolling his body over the banister, Sidelnikov, without thinking, pushed the wall away with his back, leaped forward and reached the place of the fall. On impact, they both tumbled down together in a hideous embrace: the cripple dropped face first and chest down, like a sack, painfully hitting his saviour's forehead with a sandpaper-like cheekbone, whereas Sidelnikov fell on his back, as if defeated. He was choking from the weight and musty odour of the old man's unwashed body.

They lay there as if slaughtered – for one moment that lasted so long that Sidelnikov had time to have a dream. A stranger, clawing the air with his hands, his face growing oddly young, was falling down from a five-metre height. Sidelnikov was shaking from the cold, his back frozen to the wall. He turned away and heard the skull crashing on ceramic tiles.

This mutual blackout ended with the old man throwing his head back and suddenly howling with fierce woe, and the young man hurrying to get out from under him, shaking himself down with disgust.

An impenetrable fog hid all that followed, in which the single shining need was beckoning: leave! Get away from here, as soon as possible! The train's coming…

An unfortunate delay emerged from somewhere out of the side door in the shape of a sleepy militia sergeant. They managed to drag the cripple, holding him under the arms, to a room with the sign, "Duty Attendant", and the sergeant began to take depositions from both participants in the incident. After his every truthfully-given answer Sidelnikov tried to get away, but the interrogator was in no rush. For some reason, he proceeded to cross-examination, as if hoping to discover some cunning discrepancies in the depositions. But conversely, the old man bewildered him with a coincidence by giving his name as Mikhail Sidelnikov.

'Are you relatives or something?'

'We certainly are not! May I go? I've got a train to catch,' implored Sidelnikov junior.

He seemed to sense some attributes of a bad crime novel in what was happening, and every single minute of delay was threatening him with permanent settlement in Nizhny Gravesk.

...

When he was let off to go home, he breathed such a beautiful freedom as he was running along the platform and jumping inside the carriage that smelt of hot coal and pressing his face avidly against the window – it was as if he had not just a moment earlier been struggling out of the embrace of this nightmarish station. Now he could sleep unimpeded, stretching his arm out on the little table by the window and burying his face in his forearm. He could change from the right arm that eventually went numb onto the left without breaking off the dream, in which the night was returning to its senses, the lost fragments of the broken whole coming together of their own accord. Nobody was dead, his mother was gentle and forgiving, and the one-legged old man was quietly looking with his green brown-speckled eyes, washed clean from grief. Sleeping through the journey simplified the universe by dividing it into two parts of the world, two opposite elements – one motionlessly freezing and one flying forward, inflamed by speed – the station and the train. Ultimately, the events of an entire life, blinkered and bridled, tightened up to the stripped thread, came down to the choice between stations and trains. It was only their lights that were shining in the winter darkness… And I was already chosen by that transit express in which, urged by love and sadness, I was to overcome the space and time of that huge country in order to burst finally, at full speed, into the faraway sea port. There everything was titled by precarious and long anticipation, there yphoons were given women's names, there a pack of impatient suitors were showing off their paltry male valour, there the salty air was speaking on behalf of the great ocean and there, at last, I was definitely expected. I screwed up my eyes like I used to in childhood – among the innumerable shimmering beings only visible under my closed eyelids, each one needed to be entitled to its own mysterious life and pleaded for my protection. And now it was not Rosa, but myself who was repeating calmly, 'don't be afraid, don't be afraid of anything,' secure in the knowledge that I would be heard.